I0784149

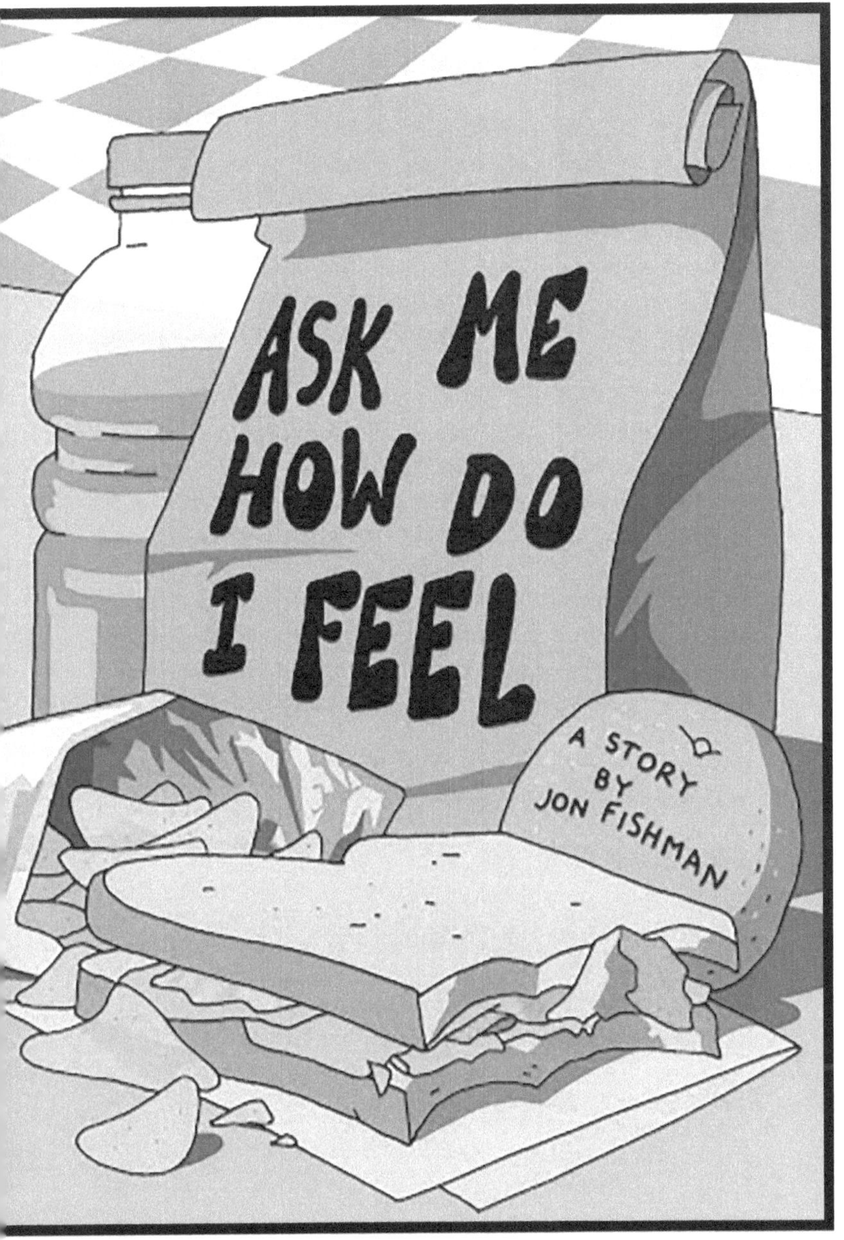

ASK ME
HOW DO
I FEEL
A STORY
BY
JON FISHMAN

Published by Argyle Fox Publishing | argylefoxpublishing.com

ISBN 979-8-89124-074-2

For Devorah Jill

Your strength, wit, and boundless imagination inspire every page of this story. Thank you for showing the world the beauty of embracing your true self and teaching us all to never stop growing, learning, and reaching for more. You are here with me every day.

ASK ME HOW DO I FEEL

1

THE KITCHEN COUNTER HAD THREE bar stools. At one time, I would sit at these stools and do my homework. My backpack would lie on the floor by my feet, a binder on the counter stuffed with my endless collections from the days, weeks, or months. My mom would cook dinner. Pots were carried up and down, filled with water. Cooking pasta.

Dad would be frantically doing something upstairs, then in the garage, then back upstairs. I would call out a math problem to him. He would respond, then look over my shoulder. "No, put this number above this number," he would say, correcting my work. Mom would give her input.

Sixth grade was when I believe I began to change. I didn't really need the help anymore. I just liked to listen to the flurry of activity making my family hum.

Now that Dad had his own place, the three bar stools seemed too much. The empty chair was just a reminder that he wasn't living here anymore. Having Mia here, though, seemed to round it out again.

My mom picked us up from school after she went grocery shopping. The front car seat was full of grocery bags. All the bags in the front seat meant Mia and I both had to sit in the back.

Sometimes Mia needed a ride home, because some days she was with her dad and on other days with her mom, who both worked until 5:30. Occasionally, Mia would go home with various girls from school. Maybe Taylor or maybe Angie. And on some days, she'd come home with us.

I stood in the kitchen feeling like I was in my mom's way. I slid past her and moved to the other side of the counter. I watched Mia slide onto the barstool. Her athletic legs pushed on the footrest and she positioned herself back in the seat. I tried not to look, but I love using my peripheral vision.

The last of the bags were dropped onto the counter. That's when my mom walked out of the kitchen, leaving the groceries to sit on the long peninsula of the kitchen countertop. I began to rummage through the bags. *Same crap.* I pulled out pizza-flavored Goldfish. In second grade, I thought these were so good, but now they looked unappetizing. Why is it that something that was once so important to you at one point can seem childish just a few years later? I could smell the "real pizza" scent seeping out of the bag. I rolled my eyes looking at Mia.

"You know she's always just thinking about you," Mia pointed out. "Even when she's at the store, you're on her mind."

"I guess." I dropped the Goldfish sack back into the plastic shopping bag. "Not thinking of the dying planet though." I mashed the plastic bag with my hand. "What else is here?" I asked, as I rummaged through the other bags.

Same crap.

"Hey, *this* could be interesting." I pulled out a six pack of beer.

"Ty..." Mia stared at me. "You realize there are only six beers. She would know if some were missing."

"What if we helped put away the groceries?" I began to explain. "Would she know one was missing if we spread them out in the fridge?"

Mia looked at me dubiously.

The first time I met Mia, I was in fourth grade. Snack bags of pizza-flavored Goldfish in my hands. Mia sat across from me in Mrs. Corman's classroom. Mrs. Corman. World's Greatest Teacher. Our classroom had floor-to-ceiling windows and at the start of every new unit, Mrs. Corman would set up painting stations for the students to paint the classroom windows. I remembered those days being the most fun. At the time, our class was working on lessons based on the state of Florida. Mrs. Corman planned an activity to allow our classroom windows to be painted by the students. Across the windows, the class painted images of long, green alligators, white-capped ocean waves, Disney World, and the Everglades. During the afternoon, the room would fill with light, and the classroom windows would shine like stained glass in an ancient cathedral. Mia and I worked on a scene of an orange grove. I painted tall green trees as I stood on a chair, reaching across multiple windows, while Mia painted plump, round oranges symmetrically placed. I don't really remember exactly how we became friends. Like so many good things, it just happened. Being ten years old at the time, some things just moved past me without much notice.

"Mom!" I called upstairs. "Mia and I are going to put the groceries away."

"What?" she called back. "I'm in the bathroom!"

"Never mind!" I looked at Mia and curled my lip.

We began to unpack the contents of the grocery bags. *Divide and conquer.* Mia knew my kitchen pretty well. She had been here numerous times with her family. Holiday dinners. Birthday parties. These days, she would hang out with us until her mom or dad could pick her up, so Mia was pretty comfortable in the kitchen. We floated past each other. Fridge, pantry, cabinet. Cabinet, pantry, fridge.

"There are *two* six packs, Ty." Mia over enunciated the word "two" as she pulled a second set from another bag.

"Math is hard. Please explain," I sarcastically remarked while closing the refrigerator's side door.

Mia held one beer bottle up. "Less likely to know one or two are missing." She continued to explain the word problem.

We took out all the bottles and separated them between the two refrigerators. We had one refrigerator in the kitchen and one refrigerator in the garage. Mia and I gathered all the bags and stuffed them into one. I hooked the big bag of bags on the cabinet pull. All the groceries were put away when my mom entered the kitchen.

"I'm sorry, you two." She looked around at the kitchen counter. "You called me and I couldn't hear."

Mia spoke for both of us. "Oh, we just said we were putting away the groceries. I hope that's okay." Mia closed a cabinet door.

"Yes, of course! Thank you. That's very helpful." Mom made an exasperated sigh. "I'm about to start dinner now. Mia, are you staying?" She rested her hands on the countertop.

I just stood watching them volley in conversation.

"No. My mom texted me to say she'll be here soon,

but thank you." Mia bent down to pick up her backpack.

Mia looked at me. "Ty, wanna wait outside with me until my mom comes?" she asked. "She'll be here any minute." Mia zipped up her backpack.

"Sure." I looked at my feet. Socks only. I had kicked my sneakers off somewhere. I looked back up at Mia and her eyes didn't blink. "Sure." I repeated.

She carefully slung her backpack over her shoulder and turned to leave the kitchen. "Bye, Jill!" Mia called out to my mom.

"Bye, honey! I want to hear how auditions go!"

Mia was trying out for the high school play. This year Seminole Creek High School was putting on *Guys and Dolls*. Mia kept singing, slash humming, slash whistling the songs in the show. By osmosis or just the mere fact that we hung out together a lot, I now knew three songs kinda by heart: "If I Were a Bell," "Adelaide's Lament," and "The Oldest Establishment."

I have to say they were pretty good songs. Mia kept telling me I should audition. She said it's so much fun watching a production come together. She and I had sung these songs together. I actually enjoyed singing with her. My response to this topic was always "No." Then she'd go on and say something like, "Well, then just join the tech crew."

Having her ask me to do this with her made me want to, but I just keep putting it away in my "I'll see" file.

She's so talented. She dances, sings, and acts. Me? Not so much.

Mia and I walked through the living room, into the front hallway, and toward the front door. She stopped to look at my baby pictures on the entry table.

"So little," she giggled.

"You've seen that picture before," I reminded her.

"I know, I just like the denim overalls you're wearing."

Mia turned back to me. I opened the front door and allowed her to pass as I followed. I stepped over my dog, Iggy, who was spread out right in front of the door. Iggy's floppy gray and white body was spread out like a starfish. "Iggy, really? Right here?" I looked down and reached for the door.

Stopping on the front steps, I felt the warm, humid evening on my skin. In the distance, I heard a dog bark.

Mia and I had known each other for so long now, that it was fine for us to sit in silence. We didn't need to have chatter going back and forth. But Mia broke the silence.

"My dad wants me to stay at his place this weekend." Mia turned and dragged her hair behind her ear. "I'm okay with that, but I think Talia will be there and I'm not really in the mood for her."

Talia and Mia's dad, Michael, had begun dating not that long ago. I'd met Talia once and she seemed nice enough, but Mia hadn't exactly warmed up to her. I looked back down at my shoeless feet.

"My mom and dad haven't started dating anyone yet." I thought for a second. "Well, not that I know of."

"I don't know. It's just weird," Mia continued. "I kinda get that people who divorce start to date again, but I am *not* interested in small talk with Talia."

I thought about when I met Talia. She ran through the list of questions that one would ask when trying to establish a relationship. Questions like, "How long have you known Mia?", "Do you play any sports?", and "You have a dog, right?" I didn't mind her, but she wasn't *my* dad's girlfriend. Talia also had a daughter, Erin. I hadn't met her yet, but Mia said she wasn't someone she'd want to be friends with, so when they all went out together, it was hard to make conversation.

Mia is someone who can talk to anyone. She never alienates anyone, so it was unusual for her to feel that way about someone.

She shifted on her feet and slid the backpack off her shoulder. She gently placed her backpack on the porch and unzipped it. I looked down again. There, between her laptop and her green binder, sat two beers.

"Two?" I commented. "You're brave."

"I don't like taking things from your mom." Mia took a long blink and frowned.

"She'll never know," I reassured her and smiled. "Can you get them in the house without anyone noticing?"

"Not a problem," she said confidently. "I'll keep them in my backpack and in my room until we can have them."

When Mia and I were in fifth grade, our families went on a beach vacation. The hotel had lots of activities set up for kids. It was as if the hotel management knew that in order to get customers to spend money, they needed to find a way to entertain everyone's kids.

I remember the options: sand volleyball, shell gathering on the beach, marine life exhibits, and hair braiding. Mia sat for hours getting her hair braided. I sat for hours watching the sunburnt hotel employee meticulously interlace Mia's brown hair with beads and colored string. The salty air and the coconut sunscreen seemed to be used as a medium to weave the strands into each knot and turn of her hair. She came back to school, and our classmates were in awe of the artwork on her head.

Back on the front steps, Mia turned to the warm breeze, pulling a wisp of hair that had blown in front of her lips, and looked down the street watching for her mom's car. I could smell the neighbors' barbecue. I took in a deep breath of the smell of cooking beef and the sweet scent of the propane from the tank attached to the grill. I closed my eyes.

"Are you going to audition?" Mia asked, not looking at me. "I really think you should. It could be so fun."

I opened my eyes. "I really don't want to be cast as Tree Number One," I protested.

Mia smiled with a closed mouth. She took a long blink again. She was scanning her mind for a comeback. "I'll *root* for you."

"Ha," I snapped.

"You should *branch* out and try something new."

"Please stop."

"Okay, I'll *leave* it alone. I'm not going to ask again." Mia smiled. "Sorry." Mia shuffled her feet and the bottles in her backpack rattled. She began to sing quietly, just a whisper, "If I Were a Bell" from *Guys and Dolls*.

I sang along in my head.

We both turned our heads toward the top of the street and saw Michelle's car driving toward the house. Michelle Kertz is a nervous type of mom. Asks way too many questions. Questions about way too many topics. But, I have a special place in my heart for her. Michelle once sat in the hospital with me, when I broke my arm back in fifth grade. I was staying at Mia's house for a few days while my parents were on a business trip with my dad's company in the Bahamas.

My dad is the top salesman for a burglar alarm company. He works for Crenshaw Alarms. The commercials have this little girl singing the Crenshaw Alarms song. The big finale is her belting out, "I feel saaaa-fe with Crennnnnn-shaw!" Her angelic face and lispy voice create the feeling for everyone who watches those commercials, that they needed a Crenshaw Home System to keep the bad guys out.

Thanks to that "lispy" little girl, every year my dad would hit some crazy sales goal. As an incentive and a bonus, Crenshaw would offer an all-expense paid trip. This one was in the Bahamas. My parents hadn't been gone 24 hours when I decided to do some fancy footwork on Mia's trampoline. As soon as I leapt into the air, I knew it wasn't going to end well.

I landed on the ground on top of my arm. It hurt. I laid stunned in her yard and Mia ran over to see if I was okay. I rolled over onto my back and I could see Mia looking down at me in shock. She pointed to my lip. I tasted blood. My lip was bleeding.

I remember hearing, "Your lip is bleeding."

I couldn't move my arm. Mia rushed into the house to get Michelle. I thought I needed my parents, but Michelle had it all under control. First, ice on my lip. Second, she secured my arm in a sling she made with a sweatshirt. Michelle scooped me up and we headed straight for the hospital. She kept my mind off of the pain by telling stories of her own mishaps of childhood. A fall down the stairs, a bite from a neighbor's dog, and a long-winded epic tale about how she got her shoelace stuck in the escalator at the mall. Apparently, firefighters and mall cops gathered around little Michelle as they tried to undo her laces and remove her captured foot.

Michelle called my parents and insisted that they not change their plans. She explained that I would be fine and that they shouldn't worry. Michelle, Mia, and eventually Mia's dad, Michael, sat with me at the hospital until I was bandaged and casted. When the doctor gave me the okay to go, Michael announced, "Ice cream for dinner!"

The continual creeping scent of barbecue wafted over us and made me really hungry. Mia zipped up her backpack with the beer.

"Oh, Michelle, how I *do* love thee," Mia sang with a hint of sarcasm.

Mia and Michelle's mother/daughter relationship was so not typical, and better than you'd expect. Mia never said anything to hurt Michelle's feelings and she never went out of her way to make anything difficult for her. Mia was a rare breed of a human in the teenage girl kingdom.

Mia and I walked up to the approaching van. Michelle pushed the button to lower her window.

"Hi, Ty!" Michelle called out.

"Hey, Michelle, " I waved back.

Mia opened the van's front door. I watched her gently place the backpack at her feet to avoid any sound of glass bottles clinking. Mia slid herself into the car, pulled her hair off her shoulders, and then pulled the seatbelt across her body.

"Ty, come over for dinner one night this weekend." Michelle bent forward and called across Mia. "You've been so good to hang out with Mia while I'm at work. You should come over."

Mia turned to me and gave two eyebrow raises as if to say, "Drinks will be served."

"Thanks, let me check with my mom." I replied to Michelle, trying not to be obvious about watching Mia's eyebrows.

"Tell Jill to come too," Michelle insisted. "I haven't seen her in so long!"

"I'll ask," I replied. "I know I'm seeing my dad Friday night, so maybe Saturday?"

"Perfect. I'll make your favorite—spaghetti and meatballs."

Mia was still looking at me and mouthed, "your favorite." And then she rolled her eyes.

"Okay. Bye!" I turned to go back to the house. My once-dry-and-white socks were now soaked from the outdoors. "Mia, don't forget to look at chapter eight tonight for Hansen's class."

"Think about *Guys and Dolls*," was Mia's response to Hansen's homework. "And yes, I'll 'look' at chapter eight."

The car began to pull away from the driveway. I reached the top of the porch, opened the door, and slid my foot out in front of me to block Iggy from running out.

Poor Iggy. All he wanted was to see the great outdoors. I always feel bad squashing his dreams. But the last thing I needed to do was start running down the street in my wet socks with a cheese stick in my hand, calling for Iggy to come back.

I spent time personifying the moment, thinking Iggy had a job interview he was late for or his long lost rich uncle had died, leaving him a fortune. And here I was keeping him captive in the confines of my mother's kitchen, while the great, big world awaited him. Poor Iggy.

"Ty, dinner will be ready soon," Mom called out. "Can you feed Iggy and put out some dishes for us? Glasses too?"

"Sure," I called back. I peeled off my wet socks and tossed them on the stairs to be dealt with later. I bent down to scratch Iggy on the head as I passed him walking to the kitchen. My mom, standing by the stove, finished the last steps of dinner, while I reached in the cabinet for Iggy's food and scooper. Scoop, pour, scoop, pour. Iggy sniffed around me and the bowl. I placed the scooper back in the bag of dog food. Poor Iggy. His travel plans were canceled and he always had to eat the same food every day.

"Michelle wants us to come for dinner Saturday to thank you for picking up Mia a lot lately." I pulled plates from the cabinet and turned toward the table.

"That's very nice. It's really not a problem. Mia is so easy to have over." My mom shrugged, as she swirled the spoon in the stir-fry on the stove with one hand and poked at the boiling bag of rice with the other.

"Well, I don't think we have any plans other than Friday with you being at Dad's." She looked at me to see if I'd react, but I didn't. I'm used to the alternate weekend thing. The first few times were difficult, but only because I always seemed to leave something at the other parent's house that I needed. I have now become, by my own design, a walking checklist. It can get overwhelming keeping track of what one person thinks one needs to survive.

"I know. I don't mind going." I thought to myself that by Saturday, auditions would be over and done with for *Guys and Dolls*. I took a deep breath already knowing my mom's response before I even brought up the subject of the production and possible audition.

"Mia wants me to audition for the school musical," I announced while my mom poured the contents of the pan with the stir-fry into a large bowl.

"That's a great idea!" Her face lit up.

I could write her script. I braced myself knowing she'd now start asking me all the information that she should probably know.

"Remind me again, what play is being put on?"

"*Guys and Dolls*," I said with hardly any enthusiasm.

"You should do it!" she prodded. "I loved being in the musicals at school! It's so much fun!"

As totally predicted, she started recounting her time as lead dancer in her high school production of *Oklahoma,* but I strategically cut her off. She went back to stirring the pots and pans of food.

I continued, "Mia is really talented and this is totally her thing. I'd feel awkward and weird. Besides, me? Singing and dancing?" I pleaded my case. "But she really wants me to audition or at least be a part of the backstage tech crew."

"Ty, you should at least do that. What a fun experience it would be." My mom looked at me. What she was really saying was that things suck now and this could be could be a positive distraction.

I sighed as if to say, "I know what you're saying, Mom."

"Come over, make a plate." Mom directed me to the stove. "You've done baseball and lacrosse and you had a go with piano. Why not try this? It could be something different and fun."

The smell of the stir-fry filled the kitchen. The scent of onions, peppers, and garlic hung in the air.

My mom is an amazing cook. I only now understand how important it was for me to taste many types of food as I was growing up. She never tolerated chicken nuggets or mac 'n' cheese. My growing palate was always sampling many foods. I appreciate now having the knowledge of so many flavors. I have friends who lived on fast food and whatever could be popped into the microwave. These kids didn't know what they were missing. I noticed how meticulous my mom was when she's cooking. The right tool or gadget inches away. Always a new recipe to delve into. Even if she found a new recipe and it didn't go as planned, she'd say it was a lesson in trying something new.

Try something new.

It made me think, I probably should audition for a part in *Guys and Dolls.*

2

As luck would have it, Mrs. Hansen was not in school the next day. I walked into class at the same time as Adam Alphonse. When noticing that Mrs. Hansen was out, he turned to me and said, "Sweet, I didn't read chapter six anyway." I thought about telling him the assignment was to read chapter eight, but it didn't seem to matter at this point. And true to Adam's character, it wouldn't change anything anyway.

I sidestepped away from Adam and headed over to my seat. Third row from the back, second seat up. I like to keep myself in an acceptable space from the front of the class and from the back of the class. Not too eager, but not a slacker. Mia walked in. She saw me and gave me the chin-up greeting. Penny Miller snatched her arm as she passed by her desk. Penny is in the theater program too, so I can only imagine that the emergency arm grab had to do with auditions happening that afternoon. Mia gave a reassuring nod, followed by a hand-on-shoulder for support, and then moved into the motherly "taking Penny's chin in hand" with a "You're gonna be fine" gaze to Penny. With that, Mia slid into her seat by me.

"I see Hansen is out." Mia folded her left leg underneath herself as she sat down in her desk chair. "I even read chapter eight," she said dejectedly.

"Adam just told me he's all caught up." I rolled my eyes. "He's read up to chapter six."

Mia pulled her binder out of her backpack. "Classic Adam."

"I think I'm going to audition for the musical," I said with a gulp and looked over at Mia.

Clasping her hands together, with her eyes wide, she said, "Really? What changed?"

"My mom's stir-fry," I said, knowing she wasn't going to understand.

"I have no idea what that means, but I'm so excited!" Mia looked at Penny and then back. "Do you want me to give you the Penny Miller Pep Talk?" Mia pulled her hair back into a ponytail and strategically pulled a hair band off her wrist and slid it over her hair.

"Did it work for her?" I dropped my head into my hands. It's out there now. No turning back.

"Not sure, but here I go." Mia clasped her hands and

began. "You are going to be amazing. No one can dance like you and I absolutely loved you in *The Music Man*." Mia blinked. I was never in *The Music Man*.

I lifted my head out of my hands, cracked my neck, and turned to Mia. "I think I would've preferred a tree pun."

Without a beat, Mia said, "*Stick* with me and you'll go places."

My head fell back into my hands. "That was bad," I mumbled through my fingers.

Class began with our substitute addressing the class. "Good morning, students. I am Ms. Sanders. I will be here today and tomorrow for Mrs. Hansen." Students slowly found their seats, gathered the items they needed from bags and backpacks, and continued their low conversations with each other.

From the back, I heard, "Where is Mrs. Hansen?" The sub ignored the question.

Turning my gaze back to Mia, I questioned her. "If I'm asked to sing, what song?" I know by heart most of the words to many of the songs she'd been practicing.

"You'll definitely be asked, but you should sing with me." Mia didn't look up from the notes she was writing in her class journal.

"We could sing, 'If I Were a Bell'," she continued. "I know it's not a duet, but we can manage it together."

"I don't know…" I said, feeling regret. "Maybe this

isn't a good idea."

"Stop worrying about what you think you can and can't do," Mia reprimanded. "We both know that life can change in a moment and what you thought was the way things were going to be suddenly are not. Why take a chance on missing out on something just because it's something you haven't done before?"

I turned back to her and placed my chin in my hand. "I'm not comfortable with new things. They make me uncomfortable."

"While that argument is very compelling, Ty," she started, dripping with sarcasm, "you should know that every experience is filled with uncertainty and anxiety, so why pass up on an experience just because you feel a little bit uncomfortable? This is a very responsible, calculated risk. And it'll be fun."

Ms. Sanders had been giving directions on what our classwork was for the day, but I missed everything she said. I scanned the room looking for clues. Adam was doodling on his desk, Penny was pulling on a thread dangling from her sweater, and the only student I could really count on to be doing the right thing was Katy Wells, who was absent.

"What are we supposed to be doing?" I whispered to Mia. "Did she give us something to do?"

Mia reached into her bag, pulled out a blue folder, opened it, and shuffled through some papers.

"Here," she said, sliding sheet music on my desk. "Look this over." She handed me the lyrics to "If I Were a Bell" and "The Oldest Establishment."

My eyes moved down the list of songs. I knew both of them pretty well. Mia had sung them so many times that they felt familiar. There was one section where I could picture her singing, the part in the song about bells ringing.

I kept scanning the lyrics and humming quietly. Another line caught my attention. One of the words was "kissed." That word stood out, repeating in my mind as I glanced over and saw Mia at her desk reading. "Kissed." The word lingered.

I looked back at the page. I began to reel in thought. I heard Mia's voice telling me not to pass up on an experience. My mind jumped to my mom's voice: "Try something new."

"Can we run through this after school, before the audition?" I was sweating under my shirt.

Mia pulled her hair band off and let her hair fall. She wound it back up and threaded her hair throughout the band again. Not looking up. "Of course."

In the back of the school, near the cafeteria, there are picnic tables and benches. During lunch, these tables were filled with students looking for a way out of the cafeteria. Like most cafeterias in a high school, it was unofficially divided up into sections. Unlike a box of chocolates, you didn't need a diagram to decipher who's who. Most of my life, I've been able to navigate through the trials and tribulations of a cafeteria. Walk in, survey the battleground, and make your move. Ease up to the lunch line with a tray in hand. I am not one to group everyone into their types, but let's be honest here: every school, everywhere has its types.

I stopped bringing my lunch to school in sixth grade. When you come to school with lunch, you're the designated table finder and placeholder. Someone inevitably walks up to you while you're sitting there alone, waiting for your friends in the lunch line. You recite the same lines. "Yeah, someone is sitting here" or "Uh, yeah he'll be right back" or "No sorry, it's taken."

By sixth grade, I'd had enough of that, so I boycotted the bagged lunch for whatever was being served just to avoid being the table shield for my friends waiting in line.

The picnic tables were empty. The school day ended and many students had left for home or headed to an extracurricular activity. I brushed off a random napkin, blew away a straw wrapper, and sat down to wait for Mia. Reaching into my backpack, I pulled out the sheet music and placed it on the greasy table. I also reached into the bag and pulled out my phone. I typed a quick text to my mom to remind her that I would be at school late for auditions. I asked her to pick me up at six. In no time, I got a response of "break of leg" and "See u at 6." Heart emoji, thumbs up emoji, the dancing lady emoji, and the comedy and tragedy emoji.

Hearing Mia's voice behind me, I turned to see her walking to the picnic tables with a laughing Penny at her side. Mia had her blue backpack slung over one shoulder, a binder in her left hand, and her right hand was busy gesturing with great emphasis. Her story had Penny at rapt attention. Penny nodded and smiled and laughed and widened her eyes. Mia's storytelling seemed to have lifted Penny's anxious mood from earlier that day. Mia caught my eye and waved. I gave her the chin-up greeting this time. Both girls sat down. Mia ended her story with, "So I never knew Erin even heard me say that to my dad."

Mia turned to me and said, "I'm telling Penny about the time Erin was at my dad's house and she overheard me telling my dad it was difficult to make conversation with her."

"She heard you say that?" I remarked.

Mia opened her eyes wide. "Yeah, I felt bad." Mia bit down on her lip. "I just don't know what to say." She bit again. "Penny knows her too."

Penny went on to explain. "Erin went to my elementary school, but we were never in the same class." Penny bent down to her backpack to reach for her sheet music. "I kind of remember when her dad died. I think it was in fifth grade."

There are two elementary schools in our town. Mia

and I went to Candlebark Elementary, while Penny and Erin went to Paulsen Road Elementary. The two schools come together in middle school and then again in high school. I volleyed between looking at Penny and looking at Mia. Mia rested her arms on the table as if to say to Penny, "Go ahead. We're listening."

"It was definitely in fifth grade because she left during that school year." Penny looked over her shoulder as if she thought someone was listening. "You guys know Sullivan Farmer?"

When Penny said "Sullivan Farmer," my mind jumped right back to the summer between fifth and sixth grade. Sullivan was on my soccer team. He made everyone's life miserable. *Summer soccer league with Sullivan.* For Sullivan, you never ran fast enough and he made sure everyone knew no one was better at being a goalie than him. He was able to point out some youth soccer transgression that made every team member think that they weren't cut out for this. Even in my eleven-year-old mind, I wanted to shout to Sullivan, "You're eleven! We are ALL eleven! No one here is getting drafted!" I was very happy when that season ended.

I brought myself back to Mia and Penny.

"Apparently, Erin told some kids that when her dad died, she was able to speak to him again." Penny again looked over her shoulder as if Erin would be standing there. "Erin would tell the kids in the class that she could talk to her dead father. When Sullivan found this out, he used that information to make Erin's life even more miserable than it already was at that time." I looked over toward Mia. Mia's eyebrows furrowed on her forehead.

"Within a few weeks, it had become a huge problem." Penny continued to share with us her story of Erin and her father. "We were in fifth grade, and I really don't remember much, but Erin was the butt of everyone's jokes and teasing." Penny took a deep breath. "I remember many days that Erin cried. I wasn't sure if it was because her dad was gone or from all the bullying and teasing she was getting from kids, especially Sullivan."

My mind drifted again. I'm not trying to generalize, but many kids rise up through their school years with scars from the classroom bully. As much as the adults try to teach us and help us navigate through those waters, having a Sullivan in your classroom is always going to happen. There's a Sullivan in every classroom. My experience with Sullivan and those like him helped me build a shield around myself. I know I'm not the norm. Some kids really struggle with dealing with a classroom bully, but for me, I just knew it was going to end. I wasn't always going to be the flavor of the week for someone. Whether it was Sullivan or someone else.

Penny continued, "Even with all of this happening, I remember Erin didn't stop telling these 'stories,' for lack of a better word. Even with Sullivan and the other kids teasing her." It was clear that Penny was really moved by Erin's situation because she was able to give us details about what had happened, even though Penny said she didn't really know her that well. Penny looked down at her hands as if to take a pause and then started again.

"Erin sort of had a melt down one day, so bad that our teacher or the nurse or someone had to have her removed from the cafeteria." Penny's eyes looked off. "Erin never came back." She frowned. Penny seemed to have ended her story. But she did add, "Erin has been homeschooled since then—right, Mia?"

"Yeah, I've only known her to be homeschooled." Mia looked up and away. "My dad mentioned to me that Talia is thinking about enrolling Erin here, since she knows me." Mia brought her gaze back. "Erin's mom never told me about this and the reasons why she was homeschooled," Mia seemed sad. "She may have told my dad, but he never talked about this with me." Mia picked up her sheet music and began to hum, stopping short. "I knew that her dad had died a few years ago, but that's all I knew." Nervously, Mia hummed again. "Talia has mentioned her husband once or twice, but not about his death." Mia stopped the humming, but looked into Penny's eyes. "I may not have my parents together, but I have my parents." Mia pulled at her ponytail and dragged it over her shoulder.

Penny swiped through her phone, and I looked over

at the few kids who were still at school standing by their lockers. Penny put her phone down. It seemed as if she took a deep breath.

"Erin had told me in fifth grade that her dad would visit her." Penny made air quotes at the word "visit" while she shared her story. "She told me this random fact and we weren't even really friends." Penny scanned her mind trying to remember more details. "I remember feeling like it was weird and creepy, but I believed her." Penny picked up her phone so as not to look at us. "I was ten or eleven and her words seemed real and with this power or truthfulness that other eleven-year-old kids don't have." Penny looked up. "I don't really remember too much."

I tried to picture a smaller version of Penny listening to Erin tell her this ghost story.

"Did you say anything back?" I asked. Penny put her phone down and I could see that she was trying not to let her eyes fill up with tears. "I don't think I said anything," Penny continued. "I was afraid of Sullivan at that time. I think I froze. Maybe I nodded and walked away."

Mia cleared her throat as if she wanted to say something. But she didn't. The kids at the lockers had dispersed. The picnic tables were now filled with others at this point, waiting for auditions to start. A group of girls stood in a corner and were reciting lines. There were some kids sharing a script and looking over the words. One was plugged into his phone, probably listening to the music, since he seemed to be singing along and bobbing his head. Some students were sitting on the floor beside us looking at someone else's phone at what looked like a high school theater production. It was hard to see. The hallway was coming alive with kids excited to be a part of something that didn't even exist yet. I heard some music coming from somewhere which triggered my brain.

I broke the silence. "Um...should we try singing something?"

Penny scrolled on her phone and pulled up some music. She said, "We can sing, 'Luck Be a Lady Tonight'."

As she found the song on her phone and cued it up, Mia and I flipped through the sheet music to find the lyrics. Penny hit play, and the three of us began to sing to the track. Trying not to let my self-consciousness get the best of me, I sang along with Penny and Mia. They sounded great. For a split second, I thought to myself, *What am I doing here?* But as we continued, I felt more comfortable with the music, the lyrics and singing aloud. *Try something new.*

3

The door to the drama room opened and Mr. Bronson announced, "Students interested in auditioning for *Guys and Dolls* must sign in." He held up a clipboard and pen. I stood up to sign my name on the paper.

"Did you both sign in?" I looked at Mia and then Penny. Both girls nodded without looking up from their scripts. Pulling my leg out from under the picnic table, I slightly lost my balance and caught myself by placing my hand on Mia's shoulder. I startled myself with the touch of my hand on her skin. "Sorry," I mumbled.

Without looking up, Mia put her hand on my hand that I was using to support myself on her shoulder. I righted myself and headed over to the table that Mr. Bronson had placed the clipboard on. There was a blue pen resting next to it. I scanned down the list to a line where I could write my name. I saw a long list of names of actors who hoped for a spot in this year's production. Finding an open line, I wrote, *Ty Steiner*.

Mr. Bronson walked up behind me and reached over to take the clipboard I had just signed my name to.

"Did you finish?" Mr. Bronson asked. I nodded and turned back toward the picnic table where Mia and Penny waited. As I walked back, Mr. Bronson began to give directions and call names to enter into the drama room.

"This is how I would like to see all of you today," Mr. Bronson announced. "Please have a song ready as well as a section from the scripts you were given to read."

Mr. Bronson scanned the list. "I'm going down the list in the order you signed in to bring you in for your audition. I'll ask what song you will be singing, what scene you will be reading from, and the part you are interested in."

Mr. Bronson looked down at the clipboard. "Also, I may ask for some of you to come in for a callback tomorrow afternoon. Please be aware, and make any arrangements."

I made my way back to the table and sat back down. This time I balanced myself slightly better than when I got up, as to not have to use Mia's shoulder as a support. Mr. Bronson began calling names to bring actors into the drama room.

"I would like to see Haley Jeffers, Daniel Ellis, and Davi Harris first." Mr. Bronson's booming voice echoed down the open hallway. I watch Haley, Daniel, and Davi approach the audition room with hopeful determination. I'd seen Haley in last year's production of *Little Shop of Horrors*. She was great. She's a theater student who can definitely sing, dance, and act. I never knew Daniel was interested in theater, and I know Davi is new this year. She's in two of my classes.

Mia, Penny, and I sat quietly waiting for our names to be called. Our conversation about Erin had changed the initial mood. Also, I realized that since I signed up later than they did, they would get called before me. I didn't say anything to them. I just continued to read over my lines and song lyrics.

"I know we stopped talking about Erin and I feel really bad that maybe I gave the impression that I'm making it harder for her when we're together, but I'm trying." Mia felt like she needed to explain. "Spending time with my dad is really important to me. I get that he's an adult and he's going to have new relationships with people other than me. But having Talia there means even less time than the already limited time I can spend with my dad." Mia continued, "And when Erin's there, it makes it harder because our parents want us to have this fast and friendly relationship. All I'm saying is it's hard to balance all that."

I looked Mia in the eye. "I understand, I do," I started, trying to put together what I wanted to say. "Have you said any of this to your dad? Have you told him that sometimes you just want to hang out with him? Just him?"

"Not like that. I just complain about spending time with Erin, which isn't very mature, but I do it in hopes he'll really hear what I'm saying to him. I'm going over there Sunday night, so I think we need to have that conversation, but I know Talia will be there."

Mr. Bronson had been calling names and many students were getting up or shuffling around waiting in anticipation. I looked at my phone. It was 4:17. I realized this could take longer than I thought. Switching my phone to YouTube, I searched for a *Guys and Dolls* high school production. A few grainy videos populated on the topic. Some looked better than others. I clicked on one high school production that posted a pretty decent-quality video. The musical began with a group of student actors bustling across the stage. Many of the actors were in period piece costumes or, let's be honest, what someone found at the thrift shop. The orchestra was playing a medley of the songs from the show.

"Sam Mattan," Mr. Bronson called out. "Penny Miller," he continued. "Mia Kertz, and Cali Denton."

Mia and Penny gathered up their phones, papers, and backpacks.

"Dammit, Ty," Mia said, exasperated. "I don't want you to do this on your own. I'm asking Bronson to bring you in too." Mia stood up.

"No, Mia!" I insisted. "Don't do that. I really don't want to be brought in like a charity case." I ran my fingers through my hair. "Go in and then wait for me after you're done. When's your mom coming?"

Mia looked down at me. "I texted her and told her I'll text her when I'm done. So, I'll wait. You're sure you don't want me to ask?"

Penny waited patiently for Mia when she said, "I'll meet you in the room."

Penny turned and walked down the hall to the drama room. We watched her hopscotch over the kids that were stretched out on the floor. Mia followed. She had to tiptoe around the backpacks, like landmines peppering the hallway.

I picked up my backpack and my phone and moved closer to the drama room. I tried to convince myself that maybe sitting nearer to the door would push me up the list. I did the same zigzag dance Penny and Mia did and found a spot to sit on the floor.

Pressing my back against the wall, I slid down to situate myself among the other kids waiting for their auditions. I watched kids bite nails, twirl hair, or tie and retie their sneakers. One girl was on her phone, talking very animatedly to someone on the other end. I imagined the person on the other end was doing a lot of "Uh-huh"s, "Yep"s, and "Really"s. Turning away, I was caught off guard by the voices of Mia and Penny singing.

Wow—they were good! I closed my eyes and pictured myself in the room with them.

Penny nervously contorted her hands and Mia twisted her hair. Mr. Bronson was watching them intently. He looked down occasionally to write a note on his pad, but looked up again. He kept his face like stone. Mia knew that this was what directors do, and Penny, even though she had been in numerous productions, found it very stressful when the director sat with a stoic face.

I brought myself back. The singing had stopped. I heard some of the dialogue being recited. Eventually, I looked to the drama room door to watch if the girls stepped out. There was some talking and the movement of chairs, when the door opened and Penny walked out first with Mia right behind. Both girls were smiling. Penny turned back to Mia who squeezed her arm and also gave her a push to move faster. Penny turned and looked down to see me sitting right there.

"Bronson never gives any information," Penny complained. "I have never seen him smile once during an audition."

Mia opened her backpack to pull out her phone. She said, "I'm texting my mom to get me after your audition."

We heard Sam and Cali recite lines.

"You know what, you don't have to wait for me." I said this out of kindness and to be honest, I was nervous for her to hear me sing.

"Too late. Sent." Mia put her phone back in her bag. She turned to Penny, "It was a really good audition," Mia continued. "Mr. Bronson is always Mr. Bronson."

We heard Sam and Cali sing. Good voices, too. Bronson probably knew that.

Penny dropped her backpack to the floor and reached into her back pocket for her phone. Looking at the screen she said, "I need to call my dad. I'll be right back."

Penny stepped away as the door to the drama room opened. Sam and Cali slid out the door. Both looked satisfied and unfazed.

Mr. Bronson stepped into the hallway and called out two other names from the list. "Allie Mussard and Joely Dudek!"

Someone from the back of the hallway shouted, "Mr. Bronson, Joely left!"

"Okay." Mr. Bronson emphatically struck her name from the list. "Ty Steiner."

Why did I know that Joely's sudden disappearance was going to push me up the list?

Mia's eyes widened and stared.

"You should go. Really." I pleaded with Mia. "It's making me nervous to have you hear...and *here*."

Mia performed the same wall slide down to the

ground and tucked her legs underneath her. She proudly said, "I *wooden* want to miss this."

My long blink was all I needed to display my disgust at the continuation of the bad joke as well as a resignation to her waiting for me to complete my audition. I threw my head back, took a deep breath, picked up my backpack and script, stood up, and moved toward the drama room.

Once inside, I saw that Mr. Bronson had already given directions to Allie. She had positioned herself center in the room and was waiting for Mr. Bronson to give her the signal to begin. I was watching Allie scroll on her phone probably to locate the music accompaniment she would be performing during her audition. I looked around the room to survey where I should sit and wait.

Mr. Bronson didn't give me any information, so I found myself leaning against the wall for a moment. I noticed that the classroom was transformed into more of a theater. Posters hung on the wall of past performances all signed by the cast members. On the shelves were various props used in productions. I noticed hats hanging up on the wall nearest to the windows. Across Mr. Bronson's desk were stacks of books, scripts, and binders.

"Ty, you can sit under the window and wait for Allie to finish," Mr. Bronson used his pen to point to a blue plastic school chair. I mumbled, "Okay," and made my way over to the window and sat down.

When I sat, I felt my phone buzz. I thought about

two things. One, I'm glad it didn't make a noise and two, I should pull my music up and have it cued.

As I sat there, Mr. Bronson continued giving Allie some directions. He began to ask her questions to help her develop an understanding of the characters in the show.

"What does the character of Adelaide want?" He addressed her by pointing at her with his pen. Allie opened her mouth, but Mr. Bronson quickly spoke before she could start. "What does this song say about her?" His pen scooped the air.

Allie waited to see if he wanted her to answer. No, not yet.

He started again with another question. "Can you make a connection with her?"

Allie waited. Mr. Bronson stared. Allie lifted her eyebrows. So did Bronson.

"Oh, well yeah. Adelaide is coming down with a..." Allie paused, "or developing a cold." Allie paused again and smiled coyly. She was making a reference to the song, but Bronson was unmoved. Realizing this, she continued, "As well as wanting her boyfriend, Nathan, to propose to her." Nervously, Allie swayed back and forth on her feet.

"Yes, Allie, I know the story." Bronson was waiting.

"Well, this summer, all I wanted to do was visit my camp friends." Allie stopped swaying and began her story again. "I go to camp in Pennsylvania, but I live here in

Florida." Allie's obvious nerves were now being projected through her long story of connectivity. "During the school year, my friends and I made plans, pressured our parents, and saved our birthday money to arrange a meetup in New York City."

I could sense Mr. Bronson was sorry he asked. It seemed as if I had spent my afternoon volleying my eyes back and forth within other people's conversations.

"We finally got our parents to agree to let us go to New York," Allie said. She was not stopping now. "Going to New York City when you live in New Jersey, Connecticut, and obviously New York is not that hard, but when you live in Florida, that's kind of a bigger deal."

"Mr. Steiner is waiting, Allie," Bronson pushed.

"Sorry, Ty," Allie looked toward me and looked back. "Anyway, the day before my flight out to New York I developed a really bad cold." Another reference to the song she was about to sing. Allie smiled and tossed her hair. "Actually, my appendix was infected and I spent three days in the hospital."

"Bummer," a stoic Mr. Bronson exhaled.

"I'm ready to sing now," Allie nervously giggled.

I shifted in my seat waiting for her audition to be over. I'd kinda had enough. Selfishly, I wanted to go, and I knew Mia was waiting.

Allie walked over to a table stationed near where she was standing, placed her phone on top of it, and started her music. "I am Allison Mussard, and I am auditioning for the role of Adelaide." She began to sing.

I watched Bronson. He was quiet but focused on her audition.

Allie was really good. As she sang to the music, I sat with my bottom lip tucked under my upper row of teeth. How was I going to pull off this audition, after hearing Allie, Mia and Penny? I should've taken a lesson from Joely Dudek. *Damn it.*

Allie sang about forty seconds of her song until Mr. Bronson put up his hand. Allie looked like a deflating balloon.

"Well done, Allie. For the benefit of time, I need to stop you there." Bronson's pen marked the air with each word as a pop. "I would like to see you tomorrow. Would you please make arrangements to be here after school?" Mr. Bronson used his pen now to write something down on his pad.

My mouth was cotton.

"Sure. I can be here." Allie walked to the table that her phone sat on. "Is there another song you'd like me to sing tomorrow?" Allie walked back to her backpack.

"I'll have a pianist here tomorrow to accompany you and some others." Bronson stood up and started to walk to the door. He opened it and led Allie out.

When the door opened, I saw Mia sitting there. We gave each other a shrug. Allie didn't read any lines.

Mr. Bronson thanked Allie and bellowed down the hall to call another student. Through the open door, I mouthed, "Allie was good." Mia crinkled her eyebrows, unsure of what I said. "Allie was good," I slowly mouthed again. Mia rolled her eyes. She still couldn't understand what I was saying.

"Can I see Matias Miri and Emma Rossi?" Mr. Bronson called.

I watched Mia watch Matias and Emma walk past her and into the drama room. Both of them did the exact same thing I did: scan the room and try to figure out where to sit.

"Ty, you can move to the center of the room to let these two sit there," Mr. Bronson directed. "Emma, please pull that chair from my desk and move it next to the blue chair Ty was sitting in."

I left my seat and carried my backpack to the center of the room. My phone was cued to play "The Oldest Establishment."

As I stood waiting for Matias and Emma to take their seats and for Bronson to place himself back in his chair, I closed my eyes. I'd practiced this song with Mia and on my own. I knew it. I knew at least ninety seconds of it. That's if Bronson called it before the song was over. I opened my eyes. Mr. Bronson was seated, Matias and Emma were waiting, and I was standing here. *Try something new.*

"Do you feel confident, Ty?" Mr. Bronson clicked his pen. "Auditions are about confidence."

I pulled my shoulders back. I felt I was slouching. "Yes, I feel confident."

Click. Click. Bronson's pen punctuated the air.

"What song are you singing today?" Mr. Bronson shifted in his seat.

I stood up straighter.

"I will be singing 'The Oldest Establishment'." *What am I doing?* I blinked slowly.

Click. Click. Click.

"What's in the way of the character getting what he wants?" Mr. Bronson asked. He looked toward Matias and Emma as if to say, "You're next, and you better have an answer ready."

Matias and Emma sat straighter in their chairs.

I decided upon, "I believe that the character of Nathan Detroit has to balance his two worlds."

Bronson listened.

"Nathan is kind of a manipulator. He has his illegal gambling games and he has Adelaide," I continued. "All Adelaide wants is to get married. All Nathan does is continue to make empty promises of 'someday' and he plays craps."

"Interesting, Ty." Bronson put down the pen. He looked back at Matias and Emma, still sitting up in their seats. "Do you see yourself in Nathan?"

"I've never thought of myself as someone who manipulates others," I pushed back.

"Do you live in two worlds?" Bronson asked.

I blinked my eyes in thought. Matias and Emma looked down to scroll on their phones.

"I live at my mom's house, and I live at my dad's house." I swayed on my feet. "So, yeah, maybe I do have two worlds, or live in two worlds."

"Okay. So you can connect with this character of Nathan in some way, for now." Bronson picked up his pen and clicked. "Let's begin."

I repeated the exact steps of Allie. Walked to the table, placed my phone on the top, and cued the music.

"My name is Ty Steiner, and I'm interested in any of the male parts." *Ugh. Did I actually just say that out loud?* I dropped my shoulders. Matias snickered and cleared his throat. Already off to a terrible start. The music started.

"Pause. Stop the music, Ty."

I walked over to the table and pressed pause. I thought, *This is where he gets up and walks me out. Allie style.*

Bronson turned to Matias, "You know this song, Matias?" *Click. Click.* "He's singing 'The Oldest Establishment'."

Matias nodded, dropped his phone in his backpack, and joined me in the center of the room. I held my phone in my hand. All I wanted to do was text Mia. Matias turned to Mr. Bronson. Bronson nodded.

"I am Matias Miri, and I am auditioning for Nathan Detroit." Matias looked at me with a tilted head and eye roll as if to say, "You said 'male parts'." I looked back at him with a hard glare as if to say, "I know what I said and I'll never forget."

Mr. Bronson said, "Matias, sing for Nathan and Ty, sing for the character of Nicely."

I pressed play. I nodded to Matias. We began.

"Thank you, boys." Mr. Bronson motioned with his pen and hand. "Very good," he remarked.

I walked back to my backpack to drop my phone inside. Matias stayed at center stage waiting for direction.

"I'll need you both back tomorrow after school," Mr. Bronson explained. "Please make arrangements." Bronson finished with, "You will be reading lines."

That's it? I wondered. *Okay. That wasn't bad.* I scanned the room looking at Matias and Emma. I gave the up chin' to Matias. He did the same. "Thank you, Mr. Bronson," I said, "I'll see you tomorrow."

"Thank you, Ty." Bronson didn't look up. "Emma, would you join Matias center stage?"

Swinging my backpack over my shoulder, I headed for the classroom door. When the door opened, Mia saw me and jumped to her feet.

"I heard you guys!" Mia shouted. "You both sounded so good!" Mia picked up her backpack and phone and followed me down the hall. "You have to stop saying that you can't sing."

I rolled my eyes and continued down the hall. "Thanks for staying." I turned to Mia. "Did you text your dad yet?"

"Of course, I wouldn't *leaf* you. Sorry…I did when you first walked in." Mia continued, "Did Bronson talk to you about callbacks?"

"Yes. I just don't think I'm ready to take on a role."

We stopped at the glass doors at the end of the hallway.

"I'm sure you'll be cast in the show," Mia reassured me.

I pushed open the door to see my mom already in the school pickup line. I waved. "Well, now I feel like if I don't get a part, I'd be really disappointed."

Mia turned to me. "I have a really bad joke." She put her hands to her mouth.

"Go for it." I stared right into her eyes.

Behind her, kids were moving through the exit doors and slightly bumping into us.

"I think you're showing some *growth*." Mia stepped back.

I turned away and smiled. "Bye, I'll text you later." I walked to my mom's car.

"But really, you sounded great!" Mia waved to my mom. "Hi, Jill!"

My mom waved from inside the car. I could see her mouth, "Hi, Mia!"

As I walked away I called, "How long until you're picked up?"

"Now. I see my mom's car." Mia stepped into the parking lot and pointed.

I reached for the car door handle. It was locked. I knocked on the window and heard the clunk of the door unlocking. I opened the car door, tossed in my backpack, and looked over the door, back at Mia.

As I slid into the front seat, my mom began her end-of-the day questioning.

"Okay, first, I'm incredibly proud that you auditioned," she said, staring at me.

I was busy looking in the rearview mirror, watching Mia get into her dad's car.

"Thank you." It came out weaker than I expected. "No, sorry, really, thank you." I gave more gusto to the second "Thank you."

"Can you tell me anything about how it went?" my mom continued as she navigated her way through the school parking lot.

"It was easier than I expected." I buckled my seatbelt. "Mr. Bronson runs a pretty efficient audition process and he would like to see me again tomorrow at callbacks."

"Ty!" My mom reached over and squeezed my arm. "That's amazing!"

"Well, it seemed like everyone was getting a callback." I rubbed my eyes. I suddenly felt tired.

I looked out the window. Watching the cars drive by and hearing the hum of the car, I felt myself getting sleepy. I thought of Erin and the story Penny shared with Mia and me.

Reaching down to get my phone from my backpack, I imagined an eleven-year-old Penny caught up in Erin's story about communicating with her deceased dad. And once Sullivan got his hands on that information, life must've been hell for Erin.

4

My grandmother passed away when I was eleven. I was about the same age as Erin was when her dad died. I distinctly remember the feeling of loss. How could someone who was just here, suddenly not be here anymore?

My family had weekly Sunday dinners with my grandmother. She would come to our house and help my mom with cooking the meal. She was a presence in our home just with her storytelling, her laughter, her soapy smell, and her soft touches to my hand. My grandmother always took my hand and admired my fingers. She was always commenting on the length of my pointer fingers. My grandmother would take my hand and say, "Ty, these pointer fingers will always point you in the right direction. Follow your heart and where your fingers point."

The car slowed at a stop light. I didn't realize that my mom had been talking.

"I'm sorry, I missed what you said." I looked back out the window.

"I said, if you get cast in the play, I will make a plan with Michael or Michelle to pick you and Mia up." She began to explain her reasoning. "This way we can make one trip out to school."

"Okay, that's a good idea." I looked down at my fingers. *Follow your heart and where your fingers point.*

My grandmother got sick and died in what seemed like a very quick series of events. My mom traveled back and forth from my grandmother's apartment or to the hospital to care for her. I would hear my mom and dad speak in the evening about any new developments in my grandmother's condition. I couldn't hear exactly what they were saying, but I understood why they kept that information from me. I was too little to understand much. But when my grandmother did die, I felt a little lost and caught off guard. Our Sunday dinners went from the four of us—loud, laughing, and plenty of stories— and shifted then to the three of us, and then eventually it turned into alternate Sundays with one of my parents. My parents separated soon after my grandmother died.

Her funeral left me with this strange feeling. That's it. I'll never talk to her again. How can one person be such an important presence in your life to then be…just gone?

For good?

"Mom, do you miss Gram?" What a stupid question. I closed my eyes. "I know you miss Gram, but do you ever just wish you could talk to her?"

"Ty, every day." She didn't miss a beat. "I was so accustomed to picking up the phone to call about my day, share something about you, tell her some family gossip, or just let her talk to me about her day."

I stared back out the window. Gazing at the passing street signs, trees, and clouds, I let her continue.

"When she died, the hardest part of all of that was stopping that routine of hearing her voice." She slowed the car to a stop in the driveway. "She was very sick, so I knew that her passing would mean she would be out of pain and discomfort, but that left me with an emptiness."

We both turned to each other. She was crying. I felt bad making her cry. I didn't mean to upset her.

"I'm sorry, mom." I scanned my brain for a new topic. "You know, it was your stir-fry that got me to audition."

Her brow wrinkled in confusion and she smiled.

"Well, really, your cooking got me to audition." I was trying to lighten the mood.

"Okay, can I ask how that is?" She wiped her eyes and giggled a bit.

"You're always trying something new." I shrugged. I felt that was enough.

She smiled. My mom catches up quickly.

"So, you tried something new." She followed my weak explanation. "Well, funny enough, I'm trying something new tonight," she said, gathering her keys and purse. "I'm going to try to make a coq au vin. It's chicken in a wine sauce."

I grabbed my backpack. "Great!" When I opened the car door, I heard Iggy barking. "I better get Iggy outside."

I walked around the car and up to the front door. My mom followed behind. Putting my key into the door, Iggy continued to bark. Slowly pushing the front door open, I reached for the collar around his neck.

"Yes, boy." Iggy jumped up on me. "Okay, Ig."

Iggy turned and ran ahead into the house giving me space to slide in. Looking behind me, I saw my mom following inside too.

"Let me get his leash and I'll take him out."

"I'll start dinner," Mom announced. She walked past me and into the kitchen.

On the front table, right by the door, sat Iggy's leash. At the sound of the jingling hook on the leash, Iggy came running back toward me. Iggy's floppy body pushed into me as I tried to latch the leash onto his collar. Having him hooked up, I reached into my pocket for my phone. Two messages. One from Mia and one sent as a group text from Penny to Mia and me. I swiped open to read Mia's text:

today was soo fun. I'm soo glad you auditioned :)

Iggy walked and sniffed as I swiped to read Penny's text:

So weird. my mom picked me up from school. we stopped to get gas. Sullivan was there sitting in his brother's car. So weird. He waved at me and I waved back.

Iggy and I continued down the street. He marked his usual spots. He reacted with a whine when he heard one of the neighbor's dogs bark.

The neighbors that live diagonally across the street have three dogs all named after American presidents. For as long as I can remember, they've always had dogs named after presidents. Currently in their pack are Carter, Truman, and Monroe. Before Monroe arrived as a puppy, they had Kennedy. He was an old mixed-breed dog. I can't remember when, but they also had a dog named Linc or Link. When we brought home Iggy as a puppy, my dad said—and I think it was said as a joke— that we should follow with that tradition and name him McKinley. That got vetoed and we named him Iggy.

I walked back up the steps of the front porch to my house. With Iggy in tow, I opened the door. I could already smell the house filing with the aroma of my mom's cooking. What was that collection of smells? Bacon, garlic, onions. There was a slight sizzling sound too. Releasing Iggy's leash, I flopped onto the couch and sent a text to Mia first.

Thanks for staying and waiting.

I was thinking. Do I text her the response to what I said to Bronson when asked what parts I was auditioning for? No, that's better told in person. I sent a reply to Penny:

That is weird. Sullivan is in my English class. He hasn't changed.

The group text got an immediate response from Penny.

His wave was weird. Kinda friendly. Is friendly weird?

"Ty, can you start setting the table?" my mom called from the kitchen.

I dropped my phone on the couch and walked toward the kitchen. Iggy laid at my feet, panting.

"Sure." I felt like I wanted to tell my mom about the conversation Mia, Penny, and I had at the audition today. "I'm sorry if I upset you in the car just now. I didn't mean to make you cry." I didn't make eye contact with my mom as I set the table.

"It's always okay to talk about Gram," she responded. "It would be unnatural if I didn't cry."

I turned to face her.

"I miss her a lot," she continued, "but I also like talking about her."

"I just don't like seeing you upset." I felt like my eyes

began to fill with tears. "I like talking about her too."

We stared at each other for a second.

After a beat, she said, "So to make coq au vin, which is a classic French stew, you need chicken slightly browned and slowly stewed in a red wine." She dragged out the last word slightly. "And a little brandy to make this a deliciously rich sauce." My mom continued like she was on a cooking show. "You may smell bits of bacon, mushrooms, and onions."

"I do."

She definitely should've been a chef. She's so comfortable in the kitchen. When I'd mentioned this to her once, she said yes, she would have loved it, but questioned whether a loved hobby that became a career would become unloved after time?

"It's my job to send you out into the world feeling like you know your way around a kitchen." She smiled at me as she pushed around the chicken in the pan. "Is the table set?"

"Yes, are we ready to eat?" I questioned.

"Yes! Bring your plate over and let's start." My mom had poured herself a glass of wine from the bottle used in the ingredients. "Tell me, what time do you need to be picked up tomorrow after callbacks?"

"I'll double check the schedule with Mia tonight, but it'll probably be the same or earlier than today." I picked up the chicken with a fork and dropped it on my plate. It smelled delicious. I could already taste it just by smelling it. Was that possible?

5

I saw Mia standing by her locker the next day. She was staring at her phone and biting her bottom lip.

"Hey," I called out as I approached.

"Hey, I just texted you." She held up her phone to me as proof.

The noise in the hallway was deafening. She grabbed my arm and led me to the door that leads to the side of the building. I tripped on my feet as she pulled me.

"What's the matter?" I spoke over the din of the hallway while balancing myself as she dragged me.

Mia released my elbow and pushed the metal door open that led us outside. The door opened with a thunk.

"Erin is visiting school today." Mia was staring into my eyes. It made me feel uncomfortable.

"Okay, you knew she was probably going to be coming here." I tried to sound supportive, but also give her a reality check.

"Last night, I tried to talk to my dad. I took your advice." Mia combed her hands through her hair. Other students were pushing past us to get into the building. Mia gave an "Excuse me, I'm standing here look" to each person trying to move past.

This time I grabbed her arm and brought us out farther from the building. When we reached an area of solitude, I looked at her.

"This is not like you," I gently reprimanded her. "Why are you so uncomfortable with this?"

Mia closed her eyes. Maybe I was the next in line to tell her she was acting immature. Maybe her dad, her mom, and Talia already told her that, and here I was, continuing to point out this behavior.

"Look, I know you as someone who's compassionate and sensitive." I actually reached for her hand. "You are the person who invites people in the cafeteria to sit with you if they can't find a spot." I paused and thought. "Oh, and in seventh grade, you waited with a crying Ava Anders when she was convinced that her mom didn't know how to get to school." I looked straight into her eyes. "Even though your mom was in the car waiting, you waited with Ava."

Mia was cooling off, but not looking away.

"What is the issue?" I questioned.

Mia blinked. She blinked again. This one was a longer blink, and then she kept her eyes closed..

"It's a lot of Erin." Mia opened her eyes. "Penny's story about Erin in elementary school is something I didn't know anything about, but I believe it." Outside where we were standing was now quiet without any more arriving students. "Anyway, Erin is here today." Mia forced a smile.

"Can we go inside and talk about this later?" I realized we were still holding hands. I let go.

When I turned to walk back, Mia called to me, "Ty, you're my best friend."

Turning on my feet to Mia, I said, "I'm about to ruin this moment with a tree pun."

Mia smiled.

"You're acting *sappy*." I grinned.

The bell rang and we grabbed our backpacks that were sitting at our feet. I swung open the door and we ran into the building.

Mia called to me, "Don't forget, Bronson's room at 4!"

Mia and I disappeared into the sea of students running to their classes.

"I'll see you at lunch, first!" I shouted back.

Mr. Atkin's English class was near where Mia and I entered back into the building. I didn't have far to dash.

Opening the door to the classroom, I slid in to find my usual seat. I noticed that there was someone sitting in it. I felt like Goldilocks.

"Ty, please sit in the seat closest to the window," Mr. Atkin instructed. "We have a student visiting today."

Erin, I thought. I looked back. Her brown hair was long and wavy. She was wearing an oversized blue hoodie, but had the sleeves pushed up to her elbows. She seemed like someone who would be hard to talk to, just like Mia said. Her long hair and her big hoodie gave the warning of "Proceed with Caution."

Students moved about the room taking their seats. I walked past my usual spot and sat at the desk where Mr. Atkin directed me to go. I dropped my backpack at my feet and looked over the students' heads to see if this was really Erin. She turned back to look at me. I dropped my eyes to the floor.

"Ladies and gentlemen, we have a visitor in class, who I believe, and correct me if I'm wrong"—Mr. Atkin looked over to the student who I thought was Erin—"may be joining us full time this week."

The new student nodded her head.

"Wonderful!" Mr. Atkin was a very exuberant teacher. "This is Erin Tracey."

I lifted my eyes and took a quick look at Erin and then scanned the room for Sullivan. Sullivan sat with Cam Baker and Elliot Kandel toward the back of the room. Sullivan was busy scrolling on his phone, so I was confident that he didn't even hear Mr. Atkin's announcement.

I watched Erin move around in her seat. She reached for her backpack and pulled out a journal. Erin had a pen sitting on her desk. She clicked it to bring out the ink tip and she started writing in the journal.

Turning back to Sullivan, I noticed he must have had some clue now that Erin was here, because he pointed to her and then spoke to Cam. By the look on Sullivan's face it didn't seem that he was making fun or had any bad intent. His face looked very matter of fact. Like, "Oh there's Erin Tracey from fifth grade."

Mr. Atkin began his lecture and class started. He was very good about bringing Erin into the class discussions without making her feel uncomfortable. Erin surprisingly seemed cool and confident. She didn't show any trepidation in answering Mr. Atkin's questions and if she was unsure or didn't know the answer, she said so.

The rest of the class moved like it normally does. Toward the halfway point in class, Mr. Atkin allowed us to stretch and move around. He introduced this time in class by cupping his hands around his mouth and saying, "Bing! Ladies and gentlemen, the captain has turned off the fasten seat belt sign, and you may now move about the cabin." Lame joke, but we were—as usual—happy when he said it.

The desk that was sitting next to Erin opened up as Mr. Atkin made his announcement. I used this opportunity to go say hi to Erin. Before I slid out of my seat, Sullivan called my name.

"Steiner!" Sullivan said in a whisper shout.

I turned back to him and gave the eyebrow-raised chin up and "I'm listening" face.

"Did you go to Paulsen Road Elementary?"

"No, I didn't." I know why he's asking me this.

"Oh, I thought maybe you knew that girl who's visiting today." Sullivan looked over toward Erin. "We went to elementary school together." Sullivan seemed awkward and aloof.

He stood up and started walking toward me. I looked back at Erin hoping to talk to her before the captain turned the seatbelt light back on. Sullivan moved toward me and passed. He was heading right for Erin. *Oh no!* I needed to step in.

"Erin?" I heard Sullivan say.

Erin turned her head around and upwards toward Sullivan. She didn't have much of an expression.

"I'm Sullivan Farmer." He actually gave a wave.

Erin repositioned herself in her seat. She pulled her hands under her skirt to readjust herself and then using her fingers, she pushed some of her hair out of her face and behind her ear.

I got up and moved toward them both.

"Hi, Sullivan." Erin didn't break eye contact with him.

He seemed uncomfortable as I stood just behind him. He crossed his arms over his chest.

"We haven't seen each other in a while." Sullivan had a way of stating the obvious.

"Since fifth grade," Erin responded coldly.

Sullivan didn't catch her tone. "Atkin said that you're gonna be starting here. That's great."

Hmm, he was listening.

"Is it?" Erin paused. She started again, "Yes, I'm looking forward to my classes." Erin tilted her head to look past Sullivan and over at me.

We made eye contact. I gave a weak, but honest go at a wave. Sullivan noticed Erin looking past him and he turned around to see me standing there.

"Oh hey, Steiner." Sullivan turned outward to let me join in their conversation. "Erin, this is Ty Steiner."

Sullivan was doing the introductions? What did Penny say in her text? *Is friendly weird?*

Erin's face brightened as she probably knew who I was. "Hi, Ty!" She stood up. "You're good friends with Mia. She talks about you *all* the time."

Sullivan looked confused and asked, "Wait, how do you know Mia Kertz?"

Erin crossed her arms over her chest now. "Our parents are friends." Erin turned back to me, not interested in making sure Sullivan was up-to-date.

"Mia and I have been friends for a long time," I said, not wanting to purposely make Sullivan feel uncomfortable, but he began to rock back and forth on his feet and look around the room.

"Mia told me you were going to visit school today," I said, "but I didn't know you were going to be in first period with me or I would have waited to meet you outside."

Erin looked at a paper on her desk which was probably her daily schedule.

"I have Spanish next period in room 502." Erin read her schedule aloud. "And then biology third period."

Sullivan and I both said at the same time, "Perkins?"

"Yeah, Perkins. Why?" Erin dropped the right corner of her bottom lip.

Sullivan looked to me as if to let me respond.

"Well, I think it is time for Perkins to pack up the beakers...permanently."

Sullivan nodded in agreement.

From the front of the room Mr. Atkin shouted, "Bing! The captain has turned on the seat belt sign. Please return to your seats!"

Ignoring his request, I said to Erin, "You actually have biology with Mia. Then, we all have lunch together, so I'll see you later."

Sullivan and I turned to make our way to our seats.

He stopped and turned back and leaned toward Erin. "I remember fifth grade pretty well."

I stopped to listen.

Erin turned back around to face him. "I remember it very well, Sullivan. My father died that year."

Sullivan's gulp was audible. "I remember that." He looked straight into Erin's eyes.

Erin sat down and spoke. "Even though we were eleven years old, Sullivan, I imagine there are things we can never forget."

Sullivan nodded with an understanding of what Erin was implying.

Mr. Atkin addressed us in a sugary tone, "My friends, Ty and Sullivan, let us find our way back to our seats so we can continue."

I slid myself into my seat and watched as Sullivan slinked across the room to find his desk and sat down. Cam and Elliot watched as Sullivan crept back over. They look at each other, then back at their friend. He shook his head left to right as if to respond to a question that was never asked. "Don't ask," is what he was saying.

Erin picked up her journal, turned to a page, and wrote something down in it. She placed her pen down, turned her head toward me and smiled. It was an "I know you know" look, and I understood.

Erin's Journal

It was my idea to return to school, but I let mom think it was hers. She began having conversations with me about how she is ready to go back to work. I took that as, I'm ready not to homeschool teach anymore. To be honest, I have been on my own this year, anyway. It is good though. We do need a break from each other.

It's strange being back in a place with so many faces that I last saw when they were 11. Now everyone has facial hair and boobs. Me too. Maybe not the facial hair.

English with Mr. Atkin. He seems nice enough, though his jokes are pretty lame. At least he didn't make me introduce myself to the whole class. He just let me kinda slide in and he just kept the class moving along.

Sullivan Farmer. He actually came up to talk to me during the break. The whole school and I'm sitting in the same room with him. He acted like... like we were just old classmates catching up. Am I angry or sad? You know how we've made a word called "hangry" to describe that feeling when the hunger is running so deep it enrages you? I kinda need a word here.

sad + angry = sangry. Easy to pronounce and understand - maybe. Am I sangry?

mad + sadness = madness. Already a word, although it does convey this situation - possible

rage + sadly = radly. I like it, but maybe for a dog. C'mere Radly! - not what I'm looking for.

Sullivan was such a huge problem for me when I was little. I can't let him continue to be that person. He shattered my upside down world. I'm ready to enter the world of the living, but not with Sullivan. Doesn't he remember how cruel he was? Or does he just not care?

Met Ty. Super friendly - like Mia said.

I'm nervous about the rest of the day, especially Biology with Mr. Perkins. Ty and Sullivan both seem to think he's not great. At least Mia will be there.

It's hard being back surrounded by memories. I hope I can make it through this year, or even this day without falling apart.

6

Lunch period arrived with the same frenetic pace as it usually did. The cafeteria was loud and crowded and filled with an oily smell. Students, like herring moving upstream, found their way through bigger crowds and arrived at their usual tables.

I'm always the first to arrive at our designated spot. I bent over the table to blow off some crumbs and sit down. This is me again, fighting off the wandering crowds of people looking for an extra chair or place to sit. Today was no exception.

"Ty, is someone sitting here?" Sullivan approached and asked.

"I need all the chairs, Sullivan," I told him.

"I'm not looking for a chair," Sullivan explains. "I'm looking to sit down."

"Oh, sorry." I was caught off guard. "Yeah, sit here." I did the mental math in my head. Mia, probably Erin, maybe Penny, Sullivan (which is weird), and me. *Try something new.* Everyone seemed to be trying something new.

"I thought since you sit here with Mia and Mia will probably be with Erin, maybe I could finish catching up with Erin."

Catching up? I raised my eyebrows. I needed to text Mia. I wondered, *How do I do this without him seeing?* "Sure. Oh sure, I bet they'll be together." As I slid my phone out of my pocket, I saw Mia, Penny, and Erin walking toward the table Sullivan and I were sitting at. I waved to them as they approached.

Penny arrived at the table first. "Hi, Ty."

I jumped up to get another chair from a nearby table. This was new. Now I had to ask a group of people if a chair was being used. Sullivan stood too. This was new, too. This "new" Sullivan.

Mia, Penny, and Erin looked around the table trying to decide who should sit where. I placed the extra chair on the end and sat in it. I would be the shield between Erin and Sullivan or Mia and Erin or whoever needed to be separated. I'd serve as the barrier.

Mia addressed Sullivan. "You usually sit with your friends on the other side of the cafeteria." She moved past me and the chair I was sitting in. I glanced at Penny who was visibly uncomfortable. I blocked Sullivan and Penny. Penny squeezed by Sullivan and sat next to him, leaving Erin to sit directly across from Sullivan.

Erin fell into her chair and began right away. "Sullivan, I'm taking a guess as to what's happening here, but I don't think I want this to happen here or today, or any day," she said.

Mia looked at me. I tried to discreetly shrug my shoulders and widen my eyes.

Sullivan placed a brown-bagged lunch on the table. He pulled out a sandwich folded in foil.

"Nothing needs to happen here. Let's just have lunch," Erin said, and shook her head.

Penny put her hands on her face. The cafeteria was exceptionally loud.

"Ty, are you ready for second auditions?" Mia launched into a conversation of diversion.

I looked up from my sandwich. "Yes. If we're just reading some lines today, I think I'm going to be okay." Since I was sitting on the end of the table, I was in a constant state of being bumped into by passing students. I tried to scoot my chair closer to the table.

"Bronson always drags out the audition process so unnecessarily," Penny nervously added. "Last year's auditions seemed endless," she said with a nervous giggle and a stuffed mouth.

"I know you didn't audition for the show, Erin, but

you should think about being part of the backstage crew. I bet it's not too late to express interest to Mr. Bronson," I mentioned.

Mia looked at me harshly. Did I say something wrong? Or did I just use the line she gave me on Erin? I got bumped again by a student passing by our table. I tried again to slide my chair closer to the table.

"Mia told me about the show, but I've never been in a school show," Erin said, sounding interested. Erin's eyes softened. "That's not all true. I was in my fourth grade class production of *The Cat in the Hat*." Erin turned and looked at Sullivan. "You remember that, Sullivan," Erin dug in. "You seem to remember a lot." Erin interlaced her fingers and placed her hands on the table.

Sullivan looked up from his sandwich. He swallowed and replied, "I do, in Miss Emmert's class." He scanned the table. He took a bite of his sandwich, waited a beat, and said with a mouth full of roast beef, "I was Fish."

I snickered at the thought of a little Sullivan as Fish in a fourth grade production of *The Cat in the Hat*. Sullivan laughed too. I looked around at the table.

The noise from the cafeteria had dissipated to a faint murmur. Penny was wrestling with trying a bag of potato chips that refused to open. Mia was scooping her cut veggies in some kind of dip. And Erin had dropped her gaze on Sullivan and began to open her bagged lunch. Catching Mia's eyes, I smiled. She smiled back.

Mia said, "I think both of you should ask Mr. Bronson about working backstage for *Guys and Dolls*."

Sullivan looked toward Mia. Erin turned to her, too.

"You both should," Mia addressed Erin. "It'll help you to start to meet some people here." Mia then turned her head. "And Sullivan, as of today, you too seem to be looking for ways to talk to people you've known for a long time."

Sullivan's eyebrows furrowed and Mia noticed this.

"All I am saying is that Bronson loves to have people backstage and you both need something to do."

Sullivan turned to Erin. "Could be fun," he said with a smile.

"What is happening here, Sullivan?" Erin had finally cracked.

The cafeteria continued to empty, and I noticed that I wasn't getting bumped anymore.

Sullivan wasn't smiling anymore. "I'm just trying, Erin."

"Mia, where's the bathroom?" Erin gathered her food and any garbage she had made.

Mia, startled by Erin's energy, said, "Just past that long table. You'll see a blue door on the left."

Penny was watching this all transpire while trying to quietly crunch her potato chips.

Erin got up, headed for the bathroom and announced, "I'll see you at your locker after school, Mia."

Mia and I looked at Penny, who made an exasperated huff and spoke. "Sullivan."

"Penny," Sullivan snapped back.

"Do I need to explain to you what the problem is here?" Penny shifted in her seat.

Penny was uncomfortable with the topic, and it showed on her face and in her body language. Sullivan didn't respond to her.

"Jeez, Sullivan!" Penny balled up her potato chip bag. It seemed to be the only noise in the cafeteria now.

"She didn't want to talk about it!" he shouted. "I know what's happening here!"

He continued, "When I saw Erin in English this morning, I was surprised." Sullivan looked only at Penny. "I hadn't seen Erin in all these years and then there she was!" Sullivan's voice cracked. "You were there! You remember what was happening that year."

Penny pulled herself over the table to close in on Sullivan. "What I remember is that you made her life miserable." Penny was getting agitated again. "It was relentless. It was cruel. Now you're sitting here wanting to eat lunch with her and join a damn club together."

Sullivan was quiet.

The cafeteria staff had been making their way around the room picking up disregarded trash and wiping down sticky tables. The smell of cleaning supplies overtook the smell of the greasy, oily scents of the cafeteria. I looked up at the clock on the wall and noticed that lunch period was almost over.

"I felt something when she walked into the classroom this morning," he said, having difficulty explaining. "I felt like I needed to say something to her."

Penny's face softened.

"I remember. I'm not proud of how I acted. I was a kid." Sullivan faced me. "I was scared."

The cafeteria has now emptied and the first bell was ringing, announcing it was time to move to our next class. Mia, Penny, and I moved to collect our garbage, our backpacks, and our phones. Sullivan just remained seated. Unmoved. The three of us looked at each other.

"Sullivan, we need to go to class now," I spoke. "Come to Bronson's at four and ask about working backstage."

He looked up at me. His eyes were wet. He nodded his head slightly. "My dad was really sick that year in fifth grade," he remarked. "I thought I was going to lose him. I thought he was going to die."

We all paused to listen to him.

"My dad was diagnosed with cancer that year," he continued. "I was really freaked out when Erin's dad died. I was afraid that her life was going to be my life, too. I was acting out and being immature."

"I didn't know any of this." Penny sat back down. "You never told any of us this."

Mia sat back down.

I sat down.

"We're going to be late," Sullivan said. His expression lightened, and he looked around as if he just returned from wherever his mind took him. The cafeteria was completely empty now except for us.

"Please come to Mr. Bronson's class at four," Mia said and nodded.

We gathered our belongings and began to head for the large doors to exit the cafeteria. Penny and Mia walk out first and faster. Sullivan and I hung back letting the girls walk ahead.

"How is your dad now?" I asked Sullivan. Sullivan reached over to the trash can and tossed in his garbage. He turned to me and took my garbage from my hand and threw it in the trash, too.

He didn't answer my question. I let it go. We walked out of the cafeteria together.

Erin's Journal

We're not old friends catching up. And Mia, is she trying to push us together? Like we're kids in a sandbox!

When Sullivan mentioned The Cat in the Hat, *I wanted to scream. How dare he bring up fourth grade like it's some fond memory we share? He remembers being the Fish? What else do you remember, Sullivan?*

Damn it. Why do I feel like I'm about to cry? And now I'm crying! I thought I could handle this. Everyone's trying to be protective and gentle.

I had to get out of there, but sitting on the counter of the bathroom in a high school cafeteria writing in my journal is making me "radly."

The radly feeling of writing in your journal while crying over a person seems weak.

The cafeteria and the bathroom smell bad too.

Students who were asked by Mr. Bronson to come to the callbacks had arrived outside his classroom door. Some were sitting on the hallway floor, some were leaning against the walls and some were just standing looking at their phones or reading over their scripts. I looked around the group for either Mia or Penny. In scanning the group, I saw Erin. She was one of the few that has positioned herself up against the wall. I walked over to tell her that I was glad she was here.

"Hi," I said as I approached Erin.

She was engrossed in her phone.

"Oh, hi." Erin looked caught off guard. "I am so sorry that I walked out that way during lunch."

Some kids walked by us. They were singing.

"It's okay," I responded. "Don't apologize."

Erin looked over my shoulder and waved. I turned to see Mia and Penny walking toward us.

Penny approached and asked, "Did Bronson give any

information on how he wants us to audition?"

"I just got here, and I haven't seen him," I said.

"I just got here too, and I don't even know what he looks like," Erin laughed.

We all laughed.

Mia turned to Erin. "I'm glad you're here. I think Mr. Bronson will be happy to have you join us."

"Thanks, Mia," Erin said. "Could you introduce us when he gets here?"

I continued watching the two of them melt the ice between them. I caught Mia's eyes and smiled slightly. She saw that I knew she was trying.

"Steiner!" Sullivan bellowed from the end of the hall. "Steiner!"

Turning around toward his voice, I saw Sullivan taking huge strides down the hallway. He was practically running. I waved toward him. Erin released a sigh.

Penny recognized the sound of exasperation. "Is this okay, Erin?"

"It's fine." Erin swiped her phone closed and slid it into her backpack. "I ran away from him once and I'm not going to do it again." She laughed. "That's not including the stomping off I did in the cafeteria today; that doesn't count."

Sullivan arrived at our small group. "Where's Bronson? I want to tell him I'm interested in working on the show."

The hallway was filled with about twenty kids waiting for directions about the callbacks. Many of the kids that were at the audition yesterday weren't there. Were the kids here just the core group of actors to be cast in the show? I turned when I heard Mr. Bronson's door open, and I noticed him step into the hallway. He was holding the clipboard again.

"Here's how today is going to work, actors. I will ask everyone to come into my classroom and find a seat. Before you sit, you will see a table that has copies of portions of the script. It's also called a 'side'. 'Sides' are the lines of monologue or dialogue taken from the actual script. Please pick up one of the 'sides' and then find a seat."

Mr. Bronson moved back into his classroom as the group in the hallway gathered their belongings and made their way inside too.

"Erin, Sullivan—I'll introduce you to Mr. Bronson." I turned to both of them.

Mia and I entered the room together and made our way to the front to speak to Mr. Bronson. Both Erin and Sullivan followed.

"Mr. Bronson, this is Erin Tracey." Mia started with the introductions. "She's new to school and is interested in working on *Guys and Dolls* with the tech crew."

Bronson reached out to shake her hand. Erin did the same.

I added to the introductions. "Also, you know Sullivan Farmer."

"I do." Bronson was resistant to shake his hand. Sullivan stretched his hand, out and eventually Bronson did the same.

"Sullivan, are you interested in working with the *Guys and Dolls* tech crew?" Bronson was holding back the sarcasm. Unsuccessfully.

Sullivan noticed, but he nodded his head and said, "Mr. Bronson, Ty and Mia think that it would be a great experience for me to try 'teching' the show." Sullivan continued, "I would really like to help."

Bronson turned to Erin. "And Erin?"

Erin pulled on her hoodie strings that were hanging in front of her. "I'm new here, as of today. Ty and Mia thought the same thing for me."

Mr. Bronson unclipped and shuffled the papers and re-clipped the stack to the clipboard. "Well, this is a big production. One that I'm going to need a lot of support on. To be honest, Sullivan, I didn't think this was your thing, but I'm very happy to have you here. Erin, welcome to our school and to *Guys and Dolls*." Mr. Bronson smiled and moved front and center of the room.

Mia and I looked at each other and tilted our heads to point to the chairs set up for us to sit in.

Bronson turned back to Erin and Sullivan. "I'd like both of you to stay to hear the actors audition, so you can start feeling like you're part of this group."

Both Sullivan and Erin smiled and thanked Mr. Bronson. Sullivan looked at Erin with a huge grin. She quickly turned around and followed Mia. He dropped his smile and looked around the room to find a chair to sit in and watch the callbacks.

Mr. Bronson moved to the front of the room to address the crowd of anxious actors. "Thank you, actors, for arriving on time. We will begin in a moment, but I want to go over the process." Bronson described to the group how each of us would have an opportunity to read for parts. He said that he might ask us to read for different parts. He explained that in all his years directing plays, he always gets it right. Bronson said, "Trust the process."

I closed my eyes and tried to picture myself in a lead role and not as a "person on a train." *Well,* I wondered, *maybe the "person on a train" wouldn't be a bad part.*

"Are there any questions?" Mr. Bronson asked the group. Bronson pointed over the group to answer a question from the back of the room. "Yes, Penny."

I turned around to see that Penny had her hand raised.

Mia leaned over to me and whispered, "She's going to ask about the cast list."

"When will the cast list go up?" Penny asked and Mia smiled.

"My goal is to have the cast list up by Sunday night."

Bronson moved from the center of the room and found a seat in the back. Students were flipping through the selected copies of the script. Mumbles and murmurs filled the room as Bronson called the first students to read.

"Can I have Penny read for Adelaide and Matias read for Nathan?" Bronson scribbled something on the papers attached to the clipboard as Penny and Matias moved to the front of the room.

"Page three, actors." Mr. Bronson gave more information.

The seated group flipped through the script to find the scene Penny and Matias would be reading. The two of them stood awkwardly next to each other waiting for more directions.

Bronson set the mood by saying, "Adelaide wants nothing more than Nathan's attention and a wedding. Nathan wants to play his craps game and he enjoys having Adelaide's attention, but he is not ready for anything more than that."

Penny blinked, and Matias cracked his knuckles.

Bronson finished his thought with, "Marriage." Auditions started. "When you're ready, you may begin."

Matias read his first line, "Oh, Adelaide, a present? For me?"

"I hope you like it, Nathan," Penny responded.

"Oh wow, a belt!" Matias started to feel comfortable with his lines.

Penny said, "Read the card!"

Matias pretended to look at a card attached to a gift. "'Sugar is sweet, and so is jelly, so put this belt around your belly.' That's so sweet. Look, Adelaide...about your present. I didn't get one. I'm sorry." Matias placed his hand on Penny's shoulder. I heard him whisper something off the script. "Is this okay?"

Penny nodded and said her next line. "No, I kinda like it when you forget to give me presents. It makes me feel like we're married."

Bronson barked out a hearty laugh and said, "Nice job, you two!"

Penny and Matias moved from the front of the room back to their seats. Mia turned in her seat to face Penny and gave her a thumbs up. Penny smiled and rolled her eyes.

Mr. Bronson announced, "I'd like to see the same scene with Allie Mussard and Ty Steiner."

"Go, Steiner!" Sullivan cheered from the back.

Chairs squeaked and heads pivoted toward Sullivan.

Bronson reprimanded Sullivan, "Mr. Farmer, we are in the drama classroom not on the field."

It was a cliche teacher remark, but I did enjoy the shoutout from Sullivan. Mia looked over at me as I gathered my script and turned to page three. *Gulp.*

Allie arrived at the front of the room first.

Bronson said, "Penny and Matias did a very good

job with this scene. What can you do to make this scene yours?"

I read the first line, trying for something different than Matias. "Oh, Adelaide, a present? For me?"

"I hope you like it, Nathan." Allie said in a squeaky New York accent.

"Oh wow, a belt!" I replied.

Allie said, "Read the card, Nathan! Read the card!" She added a little ad-lib.

I pretended to look at a card attached to an imaginary gift. "'Sugar is sweet, and so is jelly, so put this belt around your belly.' That's so sweet. Look, Adelaide...about your present. I didn't get one. I'm sorry."

Allie nods feverishly and says, "No, I kinda like it when you forget to give me presents. It makes me feel like we're married."

Bronson and a few others laughed now that they got the joke.

The callbacks continued with many combinations of students reading various lines. At the end, when all groupings and lines had been exhausted, Mr. Bronson addressed the group.

"I have thoroughly enjoyed this process. All of you have shown me your best work. And to be honest, I have the hardest job. I need to put together this puzzle. I need to take all of these beautiful colors you have displayed and make a piece of art for others to enjoy. Every one of you is a color: lightness and shadows and brilliance. When these splashes of colors are put together, art is created. As actors, your job is to illuminate. Avoid the voice in your head that tells you that one part is lesser or more than another. Each one of you, with each color you give off, will come together with another color and another color and yet another color to create a masterpiece. And finally, the artwork can be on display for others to appreciate. Now go home and rest and enjoy the weekend."

All eyes were on Bronson.

"I will post the cast list some time this weekend. I will also put a physical copy on this board." Bronson pointed to the spot where the list would be placed.

With that, students began to gather their belongings and walk out of the drama room. I looked for Mia and Penny who were sitting behind me. Mia caught my eye and gestured with a pointed finger that she would be in the hallway waiting for me.

"Excellent audition, Steiner," Sullivan whispered behind me. "You're definitely gonna get a part in the show."

"Thanks." I turned back to address him. "Who's picking you up?"

"Either my mom or my brother is coming. I just texted her." He looked down at his phone.

It was slow moving out of Mr. Bronson's room. The lined-up chairs made a maze, making it impossible for anyone to exit quickly. Copies of scripts were scattered on the floor or placed on random chairs. Once I was in the hallway, Mia, Penny, and Erin stood together sharing their audition experience.

"Allie was great," Mia announced. "So were Ethan and Matias."

Erin interrupted and asked Mia, "Is your Dad picking us up?"

Sullivan and I walked in during this conversation. "Why would Mia's dad pick you both up?" he asked.

Sullivan had jumped over all the new friendship rules and seemed to have made himself very comfortable.

Erin turned to him and launched into what she probably wanted to say at lunch. "Can we start and finish this?"

Sullivan's eyes blinked and he turned to me. I nodded to him as if I was telling him, "You need to let her speak."

"Erin," he mumbled.

We all stood in a small huddle around Erin and Sullivan as she released what she'd been wanting to say for so long.

"When I was in fifth grade, I was devastated that my father died. Crushed." Erin pushed up the sleeves to her hoodie. "He was my best friend. At eleven years old, I didn't know how to deal with my grief. I didn't have a timeline where I could look ahead and see what my life would be like without him. I couldn't compare myself to other people who've experienced loss. I didn't know anyone who was feeling what I was feeling."

Sullivan's eyes began to glisten. "Erin."

She stopped him with a hand held up. "Do you remember what I was going through at that time?"

Sullivan nodded.

"I needed comfort from my friends, and you single-handedly took that away."

The crowd in the hallway was quieting and students had made their way outside to meet whoever who was picking them up.

Our circle widened as Erin continued. "Let's not get into all of this now. To be honest, I'm kinda getting used to the idea of you being around and it's incredibly painful to relive all of this, but I will say, I'm older and I've healed and would hope that if we're going to continue to be in each other's worlds here at school, you let me ease back into this slowly and at my own pace."

Erin pulled down her sleeves and finished with, "To answer your question, my mom is dating Mia's dad."

Mia looked over at Sullivan to see if he had a reaction. He remained stoic and quiet.

Erin turned back to Mia, "Is your dad picking us up?"

Mia reached for her phone and said, "Yes. He should be here by now."

Mia and Erin gathered their backpacks and belongings.

Erin said, "Ty, Penny, I'll text you later."

They walked down the hallway in silence. I was left with Penny and Sullivan.

I gazed up and down the hallway to see that most of the students had left. The floor of the hallway was littered with papers and pencils and lost items that students might or might not later be searching for: a sweatshirt, a drawstring bag, and a single sneaker.

"You were there. You were in class with us, Penny." Sullivan broke the silence. "She was telling us things back in fifth grade that freaked me out. About seeing her dad. I'm not saying what I did was okay, but I was scared and I didn't know how to deal with the stuff she was saying. But she didn't mention any of that."

Penny pulled her hands through her hair before she spoke. "I wasn't going to bring it up, Sullivan. This is her first day back in school, and I'm just getting to know her again, too."

"Ty, when we knew Erin back then, when her father died, she told us she could see him and speak to him." Sullivan was exasperated. "Look, I didn't handle it the right way at all, but that's the part she didn't mention. That's what provoked my bad behavior. She was scaring us. Scaring me."

I could feel my phone buzzing in my pocket.

Penny stopped Sullivan. "Sullivan, my mom is here." Penny turned to me. "Ty, you were amazing in the audition. This has been an interesting day."

She picked up her bags and turned to the door. "You know, I won't take anything Bronson said earlier to heart. I'll be an absolute wreck until the cast list goes up. And then, I'll probably cry." Penny ran down the hall to exit the building.

Sullivan and I watched Penny run down the hallway. She was moving around all the forgotten items. I sensed Sullivan looking at me when I turned back to him.

"I actually heard that story, Sullivan." I looked right at him. "Penny told me and Mia about Erin and her dad's death and her ability to talk to him."

Sullivan didn't say anything. He turned away and bent down to pick up his backpack. I felt my phone buzzing again in my pocket. Reaching into my front pocket and pulling it out, I saw it was my Dad calling.

"Hi," I said to my dad.

"I'm pulling into the school now. Are you ready?" my dad asked.

Sullivan was just standing there staring down the hallway. He seemed to be waiting for someone or something that wasn't coming.

Talking back to my dad on the phone, I said, "Yeah, I'm done. I'll meet you out front."

"Okay. Throw your stuff in the trunk," my dad instructed.

"Okay. See you in a sec. Bye." I hung up. The hallway

was completely empty except for Sullivan and me.

"Are you getting picked up soon?" I put my phone back in my pocket.

"My brother is picking me up," Sullivan said. "He texted me. He's on his way."

"Okay. My dad is here."

I felt uncomfortable leaving him alone. I'm not sure why. This was Sullivan Farmer. He and I had never been friends, so why did I feel bad leaving him behind? This had been a really weird day.

"Are you okay if I leave?" I started walking backward, facing him, but walking with my back toward the door. "I can wait if you want."

"No, my brother will be here soon." Sullivan looked at his phone. "You should go. I think I see a car outside."

I turned to see my dad's car outside the glass doors of the school. Walking down the hallway toward the exit, I was amazed at the amount of stuff the floor was littered with. Paper, wrappers from snacks, and random clothing spilled down the hall. I looked out the glass door and saw another car pull up behind my dad's car. Sullivan's brother, maybe? I turned to call for Sullivan, but over my shoulder I noticed that he was not standing there anymore. I continued to walk, push open the door, and wave to my dad who was sitting in his car. He waved back.

As I approached my dad's car, the person in the

car behind him got out and said, "Hey, have you seen Sullivan Farmer? I'm here to pick him up and he isn't answering his phone or returning my texts." He paused for a moment. "I'm his brother."

Sullivan's brother looked like an older version of him. He looked at his phone and then he looked back up at me. "Is this the right spot? He said to pick him up from this building. He said he had to go to an audition."

"Yeah, this is the right spot," I reassured him. "I was just with him." I threw my bag in my dad's car.

"Dad, I need to help him find his brother. Can you give me two minutes?"

My dad tried his best not to look annoyed or show that he really didn't want to wait. "Okay. But really Ty, make it fast."

I closed the door and walked over to Sullivan's brother. "I'll go back in and see if I can find him. I was just with him."

"Thanks. I appreciate that. I'll wait here. I'm Ben," he called out and then sat back in the car.

I waved. "No problem. I'll be right back."

I ran up to the glass doors I'd just walked out of and re-entered the building. Sullivan wasn't in the hallway and for as far I could see, he wasn't down at the other end of the long hallway either. Someone from the custodian staff was gathering all the items of clothing and placing them in a box. Maybe Lost and Found?

"All these clothes just left behind," remarked the custodian, stuffing it into a big brown box.

I walked down to Mr. Bronson's room. When I pushed open the door, I saw Sullivan sitting in one of the chairs we were sitting on during the audition. He wasn't facing the door. I closed the door gently behind me, not letting it slam shut.

"Your brother is here," I spoke to Sullivan's back. "Ben's here."

"I know." He didn't turn around. He just dropped his hands from his lap to his side.

I walked closer to him. "Sullivan, do you need me to get Ben?"

He didn't move, but responded, "No, I just need a minute before I leave." Sullivan brought his hands to his lap and pushed himself up. Turning around, he remarked, "I haven't always been the nicest person have I, Ty?" He was looking straight at me.

I couldn't react or move my gaze. As I opened my mouth, he interrupted.

"You don't need to answer. I know what kind of person I am." Sullivan closed his eyes. "Seeing Erin this morning just startled me," he continued. "What I did to her in school that year was awful."

All I could think was, *Where's Mia when I need her? She always knows what to say.* I began to scan my brain to find a comment or a remark. I just stood there silent. Was that worse than saying the wrong thing?

"Sullivan," I started, "Today's been a really weird day—don't you think?"

"You asked me earlier how my dad is." Sullivan looked down at the floor. "At lunch, you asked me about my dad."

"I did." I nodded my head. "Is your dad okay?"

"No," Sullivan answered. "Well, I don't know." Sullivan shifted on his feet. "He hasn't been feeling great again. He's been to a few doctors and specialists, but my parents aren't telling me anything."

"Maybe there's nothing to tell." I was trying to be optimistic. There was movement in the hallway.

"Do you ever just know something is about to happen even before it happens?" Sullivan asked. "I mean, don't you ever just have a sense of something, but you can't talk about it because then it's real and it's out there?"

"Yes. I knew my parents were splitting up." I stared right at Sullivan. "It was in the air like a ghost. Sorry, maybe that's not the right word." I corrected myself. "Like a fog." Better choice of words.

"I can't ask my dad, Ty." He sighed. "I can't." He waited for a beat to speak again. "I don't want to know, and if I ask him, I'm afraid I'll get an answer I don't want."

I was reminded of the night my parents told me they were splitting up. It was awful. I remember feeling how awful it was to know that they were not going to be together anymore, but selfishly I was more consumed with the knowledge that I already knew. It was the fog. That's how I knew.

Sullivan snapped me back into the conversation. "Erin showed up and it all came together. My dad's probably sick again, and she's here to help me."

Sullivan's announcement startled me. "Sullivan, I think you should talk to your parents, and I think you should let Erin just come back to school."

I heard voices down the hall and knew it had to be Ben and my dad.

"Ty!" my dad called out. "Are you here?"

"Having Erin here is bringing up a time in both of your lives that was painful," I said softly and slowly.

"Sully?" Ben called out. "You here?"

Sullivan and I continued to stand in the drama room knowing people were looking for us.

"She left school because of me. I made her already difficult life even more difficult." Sullivan was confessing to his immature fifth grade behavior.

Hearing something at the door made me turn around. I saw my dad and Ben through the small glass window of the classroom door. I held up my finger to gesture them to give us one minute.

"I can't say how Erin should be acting around you and by the way she was today, I could guess she's not ready to do anything yet."

Sullivan dropped his head.

"What I can tell you is that the person you've shown me, just today, is not the Sullivan Farmer I knew even yesterday." I stepped closer and held out my hand. "Sometimes we need to decide to try something new."

Sullivan reached his hand out and we shook.

"And I think you should speak to your parents about your dad's health."

He gathered up his backpack and moved toward the door. Ben and my dad were waiting on the other side of the door.

Pushing the door open, I heard Ben ask Sullivan, "You okay?"

Sullivan slid right past Ben and said, "I will be."

"That doesn't sound good," Ben gave back.

I walked over to my dad and he spoke. "You have everything?" He looked at me like he was waiting for me to tell him something.

"I have everything," I smiled to reassure him I was okay.

We all walked down the hallway and moved ourselves outside without saying a word to each other. By the time we approached our cars, Sullivan called out to me and said, "Your audition was really good, Steiner!"

"Thanks, Sullivan!" I gave him a thumbs up. "I'm glad you'll be teching the show."

My dad and I got into his car.

We sat quietly for a moment and my dad asked, "Everything okay?" He turned to me and then back to the road and then back to me. Dad drove off school grounds as we sat quietly for a few minutes.

"Today was a weird day." I stared out the car's side window. "A lot of people I know were starting something new today." I looked back at my dad. He didn't look back at me. Did he hear me?

"When will you hear about the casting of the show?" Dad remarked with enthusiasm, without addressing the comment I just made.

I turned back to stare out the window.

"Mr. Bronson said that he would have the cast list up this weekend." As I spoke, my breath fogged up the window. I swiped my finger through the condensation. Reaching for my phone, I was going to text Mia. I was going to tell her what she missed when she left the auditions, when suddenly my dad's car swerved and my phone flew out of my hand. Car horns honked.

"Hey!" my dad shouted. "Dammit, watch where you're going!"

I looked out the front window to see a car careening across all three lanes and into the left turn lane.

"Are you okay?" Dad looked over, slowing the car down.

"Yeah, I'm fine. But, I think my phone flew under your seat." I bent over to see if I could see it at his feet.

The seatbelt held me back from moving closer. I figured I'd just text Mia later.

"You said the cast list is going up when?" Dad brought us back to our conversation.

Still stretched out, looking for my phone, I replied, "Over the weekend." I sat back up. "Mia was great. She will definitely get a leading role. You remember Sullivan Farmer? From the summer soccer league?"

Dad nodded and looked over. "I remember him. I do." Dad's face scrunched up. "Why do I remember him being difficult?"

"Because he was," I laughed. "Well, he's joining the tech crew. That's who was with me in the drama room just now."

Dad shrugged. The car pulled up to a stoplight and he turned to me. "Is this a good thing?" Dad was trying to see how I felt.

Still trying to lean over, looking for my dropped phone, I said, "I think it'll be a good thing." I noticed the phone sitting by my dad's right foot. I'd get it when we stopped.

"So, for dinner, I was thinking about grilling up some hamburgers." Dad looked over. "I could let you practice your barbecuing skills."

I smiled back. "That sounds good."

I looked out the window when I saw Dad's apartment building on the right. He pulled his car into the parking lot as I began to gather my backpack. When he pulled into the parking spot, I released my seatbelt and slid forward to reach for my phone. I saw that I had two new messages. One was from my mom asking how my audition went. She added the comedy and tragedy emoji. The second one was a text from Mia.

I thought auditions were so good!

In the car now with Erin. She's super quiet.

Should I say something?

I felt bad that I didn't respond at the moment she asked, seeing that my phone was under my dad's seat. Sitting with the car door opened and my legs turned outside the car, I texted back.

Sorry I missed this.

Send.

What did you do?

Send.

Did you say something?

Send.

7

WHILE DAD WALKED UP TO his apartment, he called back, "Ty, please make sure the car door's locked when you come up, and bring all your stuff with you." Dad had all the grocery bags in his hands while he was sifting through his keys to find the one to unlock his apartment door.

I looked up at the apartment building and remembered what Mr. Bronson had asked me. *Did I live in two worlds?* In one world I was the doting son. I help with carrying the groceries, organizing them in the kitchen, setting the table, walking the dog, and making sure I'm prepared for a weekend away without any guidance. In the other world, I sit back and let things happen. I didn't carry the groceries to the apartment. I didn't even know he had them. I'm different here...in this world.

My phone buzzed with a message.

I didn't say anything.

I walked into my dad's apartment. It was sparse although he'd been there for a year, almost two.

"Ty, put your stuff in your bedroom and help me get dinner ready, please." Dad directed me from the kitchen.

My bedroom. I was very grateful that I had a place there, but it was just a small room with a bed and a table. *Live in two worlds.*

"Okay." I dropped my backpack and drawstring bag on the bed. I swiped open my phone and typed out a message to Mia.

I'm at my dad's now.
Sullivan had some kind of breakdown
or breakthrough after you left
I'm grilling burgers tonight.
I could use that beer you stole. jk

"Ty?" Dad called out. I turned and walked to the kitchen. My dad took out a bowl to mix the ingredients for the hamburgers. He had a bag of frozen French fries on the counter and all the extras a burger would need. Mustard. Ketchup. Cheese.

"I'll set the table." Looking at the kitchen cabinets, I had no idea what was where. This wasn't my house. "Dad, where can I find the plates and the cups?" I scanned the kitchen.

"Over the toaster, in those cabinets, you'll find everything you'll need," Dad replied.

I set the table as Dad prepared the burgers for the grill. We worked quietly. I felt like I wanted to tell him what was going on at school. For two reasons: one, to share with him a story about people he knows and two, to break the silence.

I launched into a conversation about the day. I gave my dad a play-by-play of what happened in class, in the cafeteria, in the drama room, and in the hallway. He asked some questions to catch up a bit, but since he knows Mia and her parents and Sullivan, he nodded without needing too much more information. We moved to the patio where he had the grill. Dad started the grill with a click and a poof, and the flame of the barbecue grill was roaring.

Grilling lesson began.

"I like to have the meat on the grill for a total of nine minutes," my dad said, grill captain that he was. He placed the four burger patties on the grill. "Divide that up as five minutes on the first side, and then four minutes on the flipped side."

Dad taught me how to ride a bicycle. That was no easy task. I was wobbly and worried. He made it seem effortless. We started lessons one Saturday morning and by Sunday afternoon I was riding. He talked about balance and speed and stopping with hand brakes rather than with your feet dragging underneath the pedals. We worked on turning with a slow glide. By the end of the day, I was essentially riding my bike independently. So on Sunday, with Band-Aids on my knees, my wrists, and one on my right thumb, I managed to peddle my way up and down the street. Dad complained once of his sore legs from running alongside me all of Saturday, but other than that, he was the perfect teacher. He and my mom cheered from the driveway each time I passed by. Being my grill instructor came naturally to him.

I smiled and nodded to show I was listening. One thing was for sure—my parents were setting me up to be very successful cooking for myself or others in my life.

He continued his lesson by saying, "I watch people press their burgers with the spatula, like this." Dad took the metal spatula and pressed the burger patty onto the hot grates of the grill. The juices of the burger sizzled underneath it.

"Don't do this. It drains all the juices and dries out the hamburger." He handed me the spatula. "Get ready to flip in about a minute."

I took the spatula and stared at the flame dancing around the burgers.

"Okay, start flipping them over," Dad instructed.

I gently slid the spatula under the burger and turned my wrist and arm to flip the burger. The meat sizzled as it hit the grates.

"Excellent, Ty! Go for the other two burgers," Dad cheered me on.

As we sat at his small kitchen table, Dad had placed all the condiments out to dress the burgers. To make a connection to what I had just told him, he told me a story about what happened after his dad passed away. I knew my grandfather, but I was young when he died. I called him Pops. I remember Pops as being loud with a hearty, but giggly laugh. He always smelled of men's cologne and deli food.

"We had just gotten Iggy," Dad began. "Pops may have been gone for a couple days."

As he spoke, I listened to every word.

"I had such a sense of guilt when Pops passed away," Dad said. "Pops was sick, but he never shared the severity of his illness with me or my brother. I never really knew how sick he was."

Dad picked up his glass and took a long sip of his soda.

"I knew that he had become very unstable and would fall a lot. Somehow he would always manage to pick himself up or get himself up onto a chair." He took another long sip of his drink. "I don't know if you remember, but Pops was a big guy, so righting himself was a huge task."

My dad stopped talking for a moment.

"It was very late at night when my phone rang. When I picked up the phone, Pops told me he fell again and that he needed me to come to his apartment and help him up."

I noticed my dad was struggling to speak while telling this part of the story.

"I told him that it would be a better idea if he called for the paramedics to help him. I knew that I couldn't lift him and he really needed to be checked out by someone." Dad had now finished drinking his soda and tilted his glass to slide the melting ice cubes in his mouth. He let them melt in his mouth as they clinked around his teeth.

"I could tell that he was mad that I wasn't rushing over to his apartment. I could hear it in the silence on the other end of the phone. Eventually, I did get out of bed and drive over to his place. When I got there, no ambulance, no lights on as I tried to peer in the window. No one answered the door when I knocked."

"Did he go to the hospital?" I asked.

"I'm not sure. I called his phone and I didn't get an answer. I look back on it now and think, Why didn't I just say, 'Okay, I'll be right there'? Not much longer after that day, he died."

He continued his story, "One night, I remember

walking with Iggy and he and I got caught up in his leash." Dad took a napkin and wiped his mouth and then took a sip of melted ice that was now mostly water that sat in his glass. He placed the glass down and made a movement with his hands. He was rotating them around his head as if to reenact the motion of Iggy walking around him, tethering him up in the leash.

"As I was turning around, trying to get myself loose from the leash, I saw my dad standing across the street, by the neighbor's mailbox," Dad explained. "The blue house...who lives there?"

I responded, "The Deans live in that house."

"Yes, there. I knew he was standing there. I saw him. I said to myself nonchalantly, 'There's Pops'." My dad turned his head to look as if he was looking at Pops. "It all happened within a second, but I knew he was standing there. Did he come back to me as a figment of my guilty conscience?"

We stopped talking for a second. We just looked at each other.

He shrugged. "Maybe people need a way to make the loss of someone tangible or okay. It's so big for our brains to compute, that making these experiences happen is like letting out the pressure...like a balloon or a tire. It becomes too much to hold onto until we let some of the 'air' out and we're delivered these messages to find peace." Dad hovered his hands around the sides of his head slightly moving them outward to show as if his head was filling up with air pressure.

I looked out the window to process this. He continued by bringing his hands down.

"Erin was young and most likely devastated, so these moments where she said she spoke to her dad may have been a way to allow her to help her say goodbye—let out some air."

I turned back from the window and nodded.

"It is such a shame that Pops didn't know you now. He left too soon."

Dad placed his hand on my hand. I put my hand on his hand. He covered my hand with his other hand and we played that game of pulling and placing our hands over the other. We laughed at this childish game we played when I was young.

"Mr. Bronson is putting up the cast list for *Guys and Dolls* on Sunday. On the school's website." I changed the conversation for some levity.

Dad began to collect the plates at the table and listen. "You said so. How are you feeling about it?" He moved into the kitchen.

"At first I wasn't even going to audition. Mia really wanted me to try out." I turned to face my dad through an open pass-through window that separates the kitchen and dining room. "But now I feel excited about it. I have my friends there and I kinda got Erin and Sullivan involved, so..." I trailed off.

"Well, any experience would be great," Dad called out. "Would you be disappointed if you weren't casted?"

"I guess." I paused. "I think I would be disappointed." Dad stepped out of the kitchen. "Well, you'll have to wait and see what happens." He wiped his hands on a kitchen towel, then tossed it on the kitchen counter behind him.

"Mom and I were invited to Mia's house for dinner tomorrow night." I looked for a reaction. We had spent many nights as two families at one of our homes. I looked to see if Dad showed any signs of disappointment.

"That's great. Those were some fun dinners we had." He moved to the kitchen table.

"I'm sorry. I hope that wasn't hurtful to tell you that." I contorted my face.

"Not at all." Dad titled his head. "We're all trying to still figure this out." He pulled his chair back out and sat down. "We all made decisions that had to have some ripple effect. That's one of them." He interlaced his fingers in his hands and placed them on the table. "And don't think that I don't recognize that this has an effect on the kids, too."

I shrugged. I didn't need him to know that it had a huge ripple effect, but I had gotten used to it by now.

"I have to make a couple of phone calls." Dad stood up and walked toward his bedroom. "Do you want to watch a movie in a bit?"

I nodded. He turned around to see me nod, and he winked. I looked at my phone to see two messages. One was from my mom:

Don't forget dinner at Michelle and Mia's tomorrow. We need to be there by 6. Please tell dad. ♥

And the second one was from Mia:

Dinner at 6 tomorrow. My mom is making burgers. I'll bring beer.

I smiled at the word *burgers*. Two times this week. And the text about the beer. Not sure how that was going to happen, but Mia always had a plan.

My dad and I spent the next day trying to fill as much time together as possible. We made breakfast, took a walk around the lake of the apartment complex, and went to get some pizza at his favorite place, Geppetto's.

The restaurant was dim, but you didn't need your sense of sight to know where you were. When you stepped inside, the whole place smelled of garlic and melting cheese and sauces. By the shadowy light, I could see that the restaurant was decorated to look like Geppetto's Toy Shop. Marionettes and puppets and jack-in-the-boxes covered the walls. It seemed to loosely look like Pinocchio's story. Many different posters of the many different styles and images of Pinocchio were hung around the restaurant. The father-son symbolism and irony was not lost on me as we walked through the darkened Italian restaurant to our table.

As we sat down, a waitress, who I noticed by her tag was named Tori, came to our table to get our drink orders. As the food and drinks began to arrive, Dad asked some more questions about the school production of *Guys and Dolls*.

"Have you thought about what part you would want to get?" He sipped his soda through a red and white striped straw.

"I'd be perfectly happy with a smaller character. This is all new to me." I reached for a slice of pizza. "From what I heard outside the auditions, there were a lot of kids who were really good." I handed a slice to my dad.

"Thank you." He placed the hot pizza on his plate. "I'm very excited for you. This is something that you've never done and I think it could be a great experience." He bit into his pizza and kept it in his mouth trying to cool it off and then sipped his soda again.

"I'm concerned about the whole thing between Sullivan and Erin." I sat back in my seat. "She's really angry and he's really...different from what he normally is." I furrowed my brow. "But having Sullivan this way rather than being an aggressive bully is better, I think." I heard my phone buzz. I tried to be conscious about not reaching for my phone while I was talking to my dad. He noticed things like that. "And Mia, too. She's struggling with having her dad date Talia, and with Talia comes Erin."

Dad listened and ate his pizza.

"Erin seems cool and all, but she's bringing this energy with her."

"Ty, you have the personality trait to want to smooth everything over and make things easier for people by showing that you're supportive. That comes with a lot of responsibility. Sometimes you just need to stand back." Dad sips.

My phone buzzed again.

"I hear your phone. Do you want to check it?" Dad pointed over the table to where my phone sat on the chair next to me.

I reached for the phone and swiped.

From Mia:

Erin and I talked about Sullivan

I'll tell you about it at dinner tomorrow.

From Penny (group text to Mia and me):

Here are my casting ideas if anyone cares

No additional text from Penny with her thoughts on the cast.

"Anything interesting?" Dad offered me another slice and placed it on my plate.

Tori walked back over. "How you guys doing? Can I get you guys anything?"

Dad looked at me as if to ask if I needed anything. It used to drive my mom crazy when the server called the entire table "guys" when we would all go out to dinner as a family. She would roll her eyes and say, "Guys" like it was a bad word. I get it – she's not a guy, but I don't think the server was trying to be offensive. It just drove my mom crazy.

I shook my head no, but said, "Thank you" to Tori.

She dropped the check on the table. "You can bring the check up to the cashier at the front counter." Tori turned and walked away from our table.

"This place is good, Dad." I wiped my mouth. "The pizza is really good."

"How are you doing, Ty?" He dropped into this conversation.

I looked up at him and then up over to an image of Pinocchio. *No need to lie*, I thought. Dividing my time between two homes, worrying about my mom, trying to be a good son to both parents, keeping up halfway decent grades, while knowing that I needed to start thinking about college. *No need to lie.*

"I'm good." I answered.

"Okay, that makes me feel happy." Dad looked right at me. "Mom and I do talk about you and always want to make sure that you feel good about things. I'm not trying to sugarcoat the situation and I never want you to feel like you're alone."

"I don't," I answered. I thought about how Erin must've felt when her dad passed away. No discomfort of being a kid of divorced parents could match what she must have felt at that time.

"I just wanted to ask you how you were feeling." Dad looked down at his plate and then to me.

The next morning my mom texted me to say she was on her way to pick me up from my dad's apartment with a house emoji. She said she would be there by noon. Dad and I got up later than we thought we would, so having a late breakfast together turned into a short time rush until Mom arrived.

My phone buzzed. I told Dad that Mom texted me and was waiting outside in the parking lot of the apartment building. We walked into the parking lot and I was immediately stunned by the bright sunlight. I squinted as I walked to my mom's car. Getting closer, I waved to her. Dad walked behind.

Mom's car window came down. "Hi, Ty. Do you have everything?"

"Yes." I looked at my bag giving a quick scan through

my brain to see if I had everything packed. I live in two worlds.

Mom spoke to Dad. "Did you boys have a good time?" I opened the car door and threw my bag onto the back seat.

"We did," Dad said with a jovial bounce to his voice. "Ty is so much fun to hang out with."

I opened the front passenger door and slid in. When I closed the door, Dad bent down to look through the opened window.

"Please let me know how the auditions go," he said, "and I also want to know more about your friends."

"I will. I'll call you tomorrow and let you know about the cast list."

Dad reached in and squeezed my shoulder and then stroked the top of my head.

Mom began to pull away and we both waved back at Dad. I kept the window open to let the wind blow over my face. I closed my eyes. I was thinking about dinner tonight at Mia's house.

"Did you have a good time with Dad?" Mom asked.

The fresh air spilled into the car, filling it with the smell of cut grass and the warmth of the sunshine.

"Yeah. It was good. We had fun together." I had a quick memory of being at the beach with both my parents. The sunshine triggered a thought. A memory of a big colorful umbrella, warm, soft towels, and the smell of sunscreen filled my senses. I loved our beach vacations. It was a short drive to get to where we were going, which gave us plenty of time to be together.

It was okay that we drove in silence. I was happy to turn my face to the window and let the wind swirl over me. In the distance I heard my mom talking about her day that she had yesterday. I faintly heard her talking about what she was going to bring to Mia's house. The car turned and slowed and sped and drifted as I did the same. I reached behind me for my bag and pulled it into the front seat with me. I dug around for my headphones and put them into my ears. I swiped open my phone and searched for the music file for *Guys and Dolls*. I thought I probably should start listening to the music.

"Do you mind if I listen to the soundtrack?" I turned to Mom.

"No, can we listen together?" She quickly turned to me and then back to the road.

"Sure."

I turned on the radio and allowed my phone to link onto the Bluetooth. I pressed the music file and scrolled to find a song to start with. I pressed "Sit Down You're Rockin' the Boat." I mouthed the words as the voices sang. I turned to watch my mom's head tilt left and right as she tapped the steering wheel with her left hand. She was enjoying the music, too. I watched her keep her eyes on the road while the wind in the car blew her hair around. She pushed her sunglasses from her eyes to the top of her head. Doing this kept her hair from flying over her face. She looked at me and smiled. I leaned my head against the door and looked up into the clouds.

We pulled into the driveway and I began to gather my belongings from the car. Mom said that Iggy would be very excited to see me. Not much happens in Iggy's world in twenty-four hours, so my return is always a very big deal. I allowed Mom to lead us into the house and Iggy began his happy galloping around us.

"Hi, Ig. Yes, Iggy." I teetered into the house as Iggy moved around me. "Let me put my stuff down and we can go outside." That was all he needed to hear: "outside." He yelped and jumped and bounded around me.

I grabbed the leash off the front table and linked it to his collar. "I'll be right back, Mom!" I shouted into the house.

Iggy and I stepped out the front door, and I led him to the house where Dad says he saw a ghost of his dad. Iggy and I approached the Deans' mailbox and stood there. Iggy took it upon himself to pee there. I rolled my eyes at the thought of this sacred ground that just got peed upon. Iggy sniffed the pole of the mailbox and I stood there for another second, when I heard the garage door open. Laura Dean was standing behind the rising door. I quickly started to move, but she saw me and waved.

"Hi, Ty."

I waved back and said the same. "Hi."

The Deans had kids a little older than me. I had been in their house once or twice when I was younger, but as we aged that changed and the things we had in common were only that we lived across the street from each other. Those friendships ended. Iggy and I continued to walk down the street. My phone buzzed.

I have the beers chilling in the freezer. Hidden behind the frozen waffles and bags of broccoli.

I held back Iggy as I texted Mia back.

My mom is baking something. I saw ingredients on the counter.

Iggy and I walked back to the house with a bit of a stride. I was looking forward to the dinner tonight and it showed in our pace. Iggy's floppy tongue bounced and he gazed back at me. We dashed back home and he let me know he was enjoying our small parade with short happy yips and barks.

Mom called upstairs to me to let me know we should leave in about ten minutes for Mia's. I had changed my shirt three times to find one that I liked best. I stood in the mirror that hung over my dresser to decide if the latest one I had on was "the one." I sneered at myself but agreed that this one was probably the best. I flexed my arms and posed in the mirror. Ha! Well, that's a joke. I ran my hands through my hair and rolled my eyes. This is as good as it gets. I pulled my phone off the charger and shoved it in the pocket of my jeans. Looking at the *Guys and Dolls* script sitting on my desk, I thought about bringing it so Mia and I could look at the lines together. *Yes.* I rolled up the papers and stuck them in my back pocket. Opening the door, my mom called again and said we need to go. The smell of the fresh baked something was waiting outside my door when I opened it up.

"Something smells amazing, Mom," I called as I walked down the stairs. Iggy met me at the bottom for a scratch on the head as I passed by him.

"Just chocolate chip cookies. Very easy to make. Always a favorite," Mom gloated. "Should I bring wine or beer?"

I coughed as I was startled for a second. "Nah, I'm sure Michelle has enough for you both." That's all I needed was for my mom to question the missing beer bottles. Would she even notice? I didn't want to find out.

"We should go," I pressed her. Another scratch on Iggy's head and we walked out of the house.

Dinner is always great at Michelle and Mia's, even if it was burgers again. We sat around the table and reminisced about our family vacations and people we knew in common. Mia and I tried to catch our moms up on the latest movies, music and terms that "us kids" are using now.

We briefly talked about the impending cast list that Bronson would be putting up on Sunday. Discussions and predictions about who would be cast as whom were passed around the table. Mia was way too kind when she was explaining in very explicit detail about my audition.

"Seriously, it was okay." I shook my head.

"No, really. He sounded great," Mia said over me.

Our moms were smiling and swirling their wine glasses. I picked up my half-eaten corn on the cob hoping to hide behind it.

"Ty, you were great. Take the compliment." Mia picked up her plate and brought it to the sink. "We probably should take Missy out." Mia reached for the dog leash hanging on a hook and clicked her lips to call her dog over. Missy was a very old dog and moved very slowly. I took the last bites of my corn and gathered my plate and glass. I placed it in the sink when Mia said, "Take Missy outside and I'll meet you on the driveway. Let me get our scripts."

Somehow I knew this was code for the two beers that were chilling in the refrigerator.

I took the leash from Mia and thanked Michelle and my mom. I grabbed two cookies that were sitting on the counter and walked out to the front yard. Within two minutes, Mia joined me with her backpack slung over her shoulder and a script in her hand.

"Let's walk down to the park." Mia pointed with her

chin, and I followed her with Missy in tow.

I handed Mia a cookie.

The sun was still out for a little while. It sat just above the trees and created long shadows of us as we quietly walked together. Missy sniffed and trotted patiently behind. Iggy would have made me follow him. He certainly leads our walks. The park was close enough to see it in the distance. I heard some voices of kids playing on the basketball courts. Mia and I walked into the park and circled around until we found a bench to sit on. Mia took the leash from me and tied it to the bench. Missy knew that this was her cue to rest here. Mia placed the backpack between her feet and unzipped it. Between a towel that was used as a noise silencer, she pulled out two beers. She handed me one.

"We should make a toast," I said and then paused. "What should we toast?"

We laughed.

"Um, how about just a toast to us?" Mia remarked. We raised our bottles and clinked them together. We hadn't even opened them yet. So we laughed as we twisted off the caps. We clinked the bottles again and took a sip.

Mia winced. "It's okay." She looked at the bottle and then she took another sip.

"It's fine." I took a second sip. We both turned and looked over at the setting sun moving beneath the trees. Clouds sat thin and long across the sky.

"Erin told me she's really going to try to make Sullivan feel like he can apologize. She told me she doesn't want to be the person who holds up any kind of roadblock for someone who wants to change." Mia nodded to show she agreed with Erin. "She said she wished she had a friend who supported her at the time her dad died. It would have made things easier for her. So, she decided that she will be that person for Sullivan." Mia's eyes widened. "If he's looking for a friend, she said she's okay with being that person."

"That's a really huge and confident decision." I nodded my head.

Mia smiled.

Mia returned, "I feel like things are going to change." She waited for my reply.

"If you're talking about what happened at school on Friday and what you're telling me now about Erin, there are some definite changes happening," I agreed with her.

The sun continued to set behind the trees.

"Yeah, but I feel like change is coming for my dad and Talia and Erin and Sullivan and us." Mia turned back to the trees.

Us? Missy shuffled under our feet and repositioned herself closer to Mia.

"Us?" I was curious what she meant by that.

Mia reached down to pat Missy and slid closer to me. We both took another sip of the beer that we really didn't think was all that great. I turned myself closer, too.

Mia explained, and I listened. "We know each other better than anyone else. You're the first person I look for in the morning at school and the last person I text at night." She took another sip from her beer.

I needed to say something too. I sipped the awful beer instead.

"I really like spending time with you." Mia looked at me.

I brought the bottle down. "I've always really liked spending time with you."

We leaned in and kissed. We pulled back. We looked at each other and then kissed again. When we separated, I took a sip of my beer again and laughed.

"This beer is terrible and yes, things are definitely going to change."

Mia laughed, too. I looked down and realized the shirt I decided to wear was a good choice.

"You know, I wanted to kiss you the day we were standing outside of school talking about Erin's first day and I tried talking you off the ledge and all of that and I knew I couldn't at that moment, but I wanted to." I was rambling and Mia was smiling.

She just listened and then moved in to kiss me again. And we did. And when we stopped and looked into each other's eyes, we kissed again.

At this point, Missy was up and trying to pull herself

from the bench, but because she was tied to it, she just whimpered.

"We probably should head back, but I want to stay here. But we should probably head back." I was rambling again. I think the beer was affecting my speech.

I took Mia's hand and we walked through the park. The kids on the court were gone. We took the last sips of our beers and dropped the bottles in a garbage can. We continued back to her house hand in hand, with Missy shuffling along.

Standing outside Mia's front door, with Missy between us at our feet, we kissed.

"Now how're we supposed to sit with our mothers?" I laughed at the thought.

As we walked back into the house, we heard our moms laughing. This made us smile.

Erin's Journal

After all these years of anger and hurt, am I really going to give Sullivan a chance? A chance to apologize? When Dad died, I felt so alone. No one knew how to act around me. My mom tried, but she was grieving too. Other parents and teachers and family members tried. But I had a calmness to myself because I wasn't afraid. I still had my dad and that was hard to explain to others when they didn't have him. Going back to school after he died, on paper, seemed right. Get Erin back to some kind of normalcy. Erin needs to have a routine. *The early days when my dad had just died drove my mom to her bed. Lights off, door closed, and silence from her bedroom. As I stood at her door, my hand just floating over the doorknob, and I could see my dad standing by my bedroom door. He would put his pointer finger to his mouth and close his eyes. I drew my hand back and walked away. I had my dad with me and she didn't. I had time with him as if he was healthy and happy. His visits with me filled my days with possibilities. Those dark days behind my parents' bedroom door eventually ended as my mom emerged and agreed that sending me back to school would bring back the schedule we were both used to. I was looking for someone to share my experiences with about my dad's visits. My classmates who were part of my everyday life had sent me cards of condolences and wrote letters and drew pictures showing their care and concern as they anxiously waited for my return. When I did return and shared my visits from my dad with the kids at school, I probably should've known that I was scaring them. They knew my dad had died and I'm telling them all about my daily visits and conversations I was having with him. But I wasn't scared, so why would they be? I would tell anybody who I could talk to that he was visiting me.*

I tried so hard to ignore what was being said, but it felt like their words stuck to me no matter what I did. Teachers, guidance counselors, my mom—I tried to get them to hear me. I could tell that they thought this was weird. I was eleven. Ugh!

Those memories still sting. The constant whispers, the cruel jokes about my ghost dad. It was relentless. Every day felt like a battle, just trying to make it through without breaking down. But Sullivan was the most aggressive with his name-calling. "Ghost Girl" and "Eerie Erin." Every time I tried to talk about what I could hear or feel, Sullivan pretended to talk like a ghost in ridiculous voices, oohing and aahing as everyone laughed. I remember the day I finally left school. Sullivan had taped a picture of a cartoon ghost to my desk with "Erin's Dad" written on it. That was it. I couldn't take it anymore. I ripped off the picture, started crying and sobbing, and probably some kind of mental snap—Mom's, not mine—pushed her to keep me home. The pain was just too much for her, too.

She quickly figured out how to homeschool a daughter who was seeing ghosts. But now, looking back, I realize how much I needed a friend then. Someone to just be there, to listen. And maybe, just maybe, Sullivan needs that now. But can I be that person for him? If he's genuinely trying to change, to apologize, I don't want to be the one standing in his way. It's not about forgetting what happened. It's about giving both of us a chance to move forward. I told Mia about this, and I could see the surprise in her eyes. I'm sure she thinks I'm crazy. Maybe I am. But there's something empowering about choosing to be the bigger person, to offer the kindness I wish I'd received back then. It's strange, but I feel like I'm standing on the edge of something new. It won't erase the past, but it might just help shape a better future. But for the first time in a long while, I feel like I'm in control of my own story. It's not for him, really. It's for me.

I woke up Sunday morning with so many thoughts bouncing around my brain. I rolled over to look at my phone. I checked the time and saw a message from Mia and a group text from Penny. I thought to myself that Penny must've been up all night waiting for today's cast list to go up. I swiped open a message from Mia that arrived after midnight.

GM Cast list day!

I texted back.

I had fun last night

I swiped Penny's text message open.

Literally dying and good morning

I continued rolling over so my feet were now touching my bedroom floor. Running my fingers through my hair, I heard my phone buzz. A text from Mia.

me too 🖤

I opened up my bedroom door and found Iggy sitting there. He sprang to life and immediately walked up to me, wagging his tail and sniffing my feet. I stopped at the bathroom first to pee as Iggy sat outside the bathroom door.

"Okay, Let's get something to eat, Ig." I reached for his head as he led us all the way down the hallway and then down the stairs and into the kitchen.

I filled a bowl of cereal and poured myself some orange juice. I sprinkled some of Iggy's kibble into his bowl. We enjoyed our breakfasts together. My mind wandered over the sound of Iggy slurping at his food.

I'd known Mia for such a long time that the period of getting to know each other seemed unnecessary. I know all of her likes and dislikes. I know what music will get her dancing, what food she'll go back to for seconds, and where she sees herself in the future. We've talked all about this.

I thought about Mia and what happened last night and wondered, *How will this change the dynamic of this new group that's forming at school?* Sullivan was already confused that Mia's dad and Erin's mom were dating. That seemed to be a lot for him to wrap his head around.

Penny was going to be like, "Wait, what?" Unless this was something Mia and Penny had discussed already.

I was deep in thinking and processing and crunching on my cereal when my mom walked into the kitchen and startled me.

She kissed me on the top of my head. "Good morning, Ty." Mom pressed the button on the coffeemaker and pulled out a mug. "Any news on when the cast list will go up? I know you must be so excited."

The brewing of the coffeemaker added to the symphony of the kitchen.

"No news, but my phone has been blowing up with speculation." I held up my phone to show her. "Penny is about to lose it."

I'd never been in a school production before, but what Mia and Penny had told me was that Mr. Bronson was always on time and very direct. "I think we should hear by this afternoon, so everyone can be ready for rehearsal to start tomorrow after school."

"Oh, right," Mom registered a thought. "I'll talk to Michelle about making a pickup schedule."

I finished my cereal, gulped down my orange juice, and rinsed the dishes in the sink. I slipped past my mom to go back upstairs to work on some homework that I never got to while I was at my dad's apartment. When I got back upstairs, I stopped in the bathroom to brush my teeth and pee. I washed my hands, splashed water on my face, dried off, and went back to my room. I flopped on my bed. I thought I should text Mia something. What could be cool, but not weird? This was all very new. I'll just say that.

> I'm trying to think of something to text you that isn't weird.
> Last night was great!
> I'm looking forward to rehearsals.
> What do we tell people? What are we?

I watch for the three bubbles to appear. Nothing. Maybe Mia wasn't up yet? I reached over to my backpack and pulled out my script and my literature book from Atkin's class. While I flipped through the book looking for the section he wanted us to read, my mom called from upstairs.

"Ty, I'm taking Iggy for a walk!" she shouted.

"Okay!" I called back. Skimming the book, I commented to myself that I had no idea what I was supposed to read for his class. I thought about texting Penny and not Mia. Why was I all of a sudden afraid to text Mia? She had been the one I always texted first. I hoped this wouldn't change us. *Try new things.* I heard my phone buzz. Mia texted me.

> We tell people we're hanging out now. 😍

Penny has a theory that the list will be up by 11:30. I turned to look at the clock and it read 10:16 a.m. I rummaged around in my backpack for my headphones. Sticking them in my ears, I searched my phone for the soundtrack. Music was playing and I was still not sure what I was supposed to read for class. I texted Mia.

What are we reading in Atkin's class?

I listened from the start of the show.

Read page 124-128 the poetry section

Flipping to page 124, I saw the title of the first poem Mr. Atkin wanted us to read. "Alone" by Maya Angelou.

I read the poem and paused, remembering what Mr. Atkins always said: "You have to read a poem twice to really understand it…to let it sink in." So I went back and read it again. The poem was brief but powerful, and it ended with the line, "But nobody can make it out here alone."

I stopped at that line and turned to look out my window. From where I was lying, I could see the top of trees in my yard. I saw a cloud moving its way across the sky. And then I heard my mom come back into the house with Iggy.

"I'm back!" Mom called up the stairs.

"Okay," I called to my bedroom door and turned back to the next stanza. My phone buzzed again.

Anything from Bronson, yet?

No!

I turned back to the book.

My phone buzzed and brought me back. I sat up in bed and reached over to my phone sitting on my nightstand. Penny texted the group.

Cast list is up!

I haven't looked yet.

Text back after you look.

I put my phone back on the nightstand...upside down. I didn't want to see anyone's texts yet. I pulled my laptop up and clicked on the link Mr. Bronson sent us to look at the cast list.

Guys and Dolls Cast Members,

What can I say other than, THANK YOU to all of the actors who auditioned for *Guys and Dolls*. Each and every one of you came in and blew me away!

If you've been in a production with me before or this is your first time, you'll know that I spend countless hours putting people in roles I think will show off their talents best, which will then create an outstanding show.

I'm so excited to begin this journey with all of you as we bring the characters of *Guys and Dolls* to life. Get ready to share a wonderful story involving the unlikeliest of Manhattan's pairings: a high-rolling gambler and an austere clergyperson, a glitzy showgirl dreaming of an honest life and a crap game manager who is anything but honest.

A couple of things to keep in mind:

Just because a character does not have lines in a scene does not mean they aren't in it. I have added characters to scenes to increase stage time for the actors. Everyone will sing and everyone will dance. Please consult the schedule for when you are called to rehearsal!

Please bring a pencil and highlighter to each rehearsal. You will be responsible for keeping track of any notes that I give you. We will discuss rehearsal attire on Monday, our first full cast rehearsal. For Monday (tomorrow), dress comfortably. And of course bring your positive attitudes! We will begin rehearsal tomorrow in the drama room at 4:00 p.m.

Full scripts will be handed out tomorrow. I will also have music tracks available to download. See me if you need this. If there are any conflicts of dates, please let me know as soon as you know, so I can make note of your attendance.

Okay, so now that you're "cozy and clinging" (Don't know the reference? Better look it up!), below you will find the cast in order of appearance. Congratulations and have a wonderful day!

The email ended with a list of the cast for the play. Staring at the cast list made me think of a tree pun. Was I *barking* up the wrong tree? I was stunned at the cast list. I couldn't believe that I'd been cast as a lead character. Nathan Detroit. I heard my phone buzzing. The character of Nathan Detroit was a major character with songs and stage time. I turned to look out the window. My phone and my head were both buzzing.

A text popped up from Allie, immediately!

Did you see? You're Nathan Detroit! Wow! Ok?

Next, another message from Penny.

Dude, Nathan Detroit! Nathan Detroit!
You're basically running the whole show. The whole show!

I stared at my phone, barely able to process it. My phone buzzed again. Then Mia texted me.

Congrats! I knew you'd get Nathan! Can't wait to see you in action.

I took a shaky breath, rereading the cast list.
Matias Miri - Sky Masterson
Mia Hertz - Sarah Brown
Ty Steiner - Nathan Detroit
Allie Mussard - Miss Adelaide
Penny Miller - General Cartwritgh
Daniel Ellis - Lt. Brannigan
Sam Mattan - Nicely Nicely Johnson
I typed back to Mia, my fingers trembling.

Thanks. I'm freaking out a little. Is this real?

Almost instantly, Mia replied.

It's real. And you're going to crush it. ♥

10

WHEN WE ALL ARRIVED AT school the next day, many of us had already debriefed via texting the night before. We were all excited about starting rehearsals. Penny was a little disappointed with her part but soon realized that she would make a great General Cartwright. The character of Matilda Cartwright was perfect for Penny. The character is powerful and motherly and unstoppable, words I would also use to describe Penny. By 4 o'clock that afternoon, we had all watched some videos of other schools' productions. Some were better than others. Some were painful to watch, but all the videos of Nathan Detroit had actors who were really talented.

I arrived at Mr. Bronson's room before anyone else. Mr. Bronson was arranging chairs in a circle around the center of the classroom when I entered and interrupted his process.

"Hey, Ty." Bronson looked up.

"Am I too early? Do you want me to wait outside?" I pointed back to the door.

"Not at all. You can help me get these chairs placed before the others arrive." He pointed to the chairs waiting to be placed into the circle.

"I'm sure you're really excited to portray Nathan Detroit." Bronson didn't make eye contact.

"I'm very excited. Thank you for casting me in that role." I carried a chair to the circle.

"Your audition impressed me. And not only that, I liked how you answered the questions asked about living in two worlds. Very thoughtful and very honest." Bronson stopped and looked at me.

"Well, I never auditioned for a play before and I wasn't even sure that I was going to do it, even up until the moment I was standing outside on the day of the audition." I grabbed another chair. "But when you asked me that question about living in two worlds, that's exactly how I felt or how it needed to be answered."

Mr. Bronson waved to someone outside his classroom as a gesture to come in. "I am very excited that you decided to audition and to see what you can do with the character of Nathan Detroit."

Others began to enter the classroom and take seats

around the circle of chairs. Sullivan walked in, as did Mia and Penny. I waved them over to the seats nearest to me. Erin walked in right behind with many of the other cast members.

The room filled with a creative energy. You could feel the excitement as if it was tangible. Mia sat down next to me and Erin sat on the other side. Mia pulled her leg underneath her. She used me as a support to balance herself as she moved into her chair.

"Hi." Mia stared at me.

I smiled back and said, "Hi."

Penny plopped herself next to Mia and launched into a very animated conversation about her math quiz. All I could hear was something about things that were on her quiz that weren't anywhere on the study guide she reviewed.

"Oh, sorry. Were you and Ty talking?" Penny caught herself. Did she know about us yet?

Mia laughed and said, "That's okay. You should talk to Miss Morgan."

Penny rolled her eyes, reached into her backpack, and pulled out her highlighters. Of course she had a new pack of six highlighters in colors of pink, green, and yellow. She opened the pack and leaned forward, outstretching an arm to Mia, Erin, and me. We all graciously declined as we had our own highlighters. Sullivan reached into Penny's pack and took a green highlighter.

"Thanks, Penny. I forgot mine." Sullivan slid back into his seat as Penny turned to Mia and rolled her eyes.

I heard Erin scoff.

Mr. Bronson stood center in the circle of chairs. The cast quietly began to draw attention to Bronson as he walked around the circle.

"Today begins a very important day. We begin to tell this wonderful story called *Guys and Dolls*. Many of you have stopped by today with excitement. Some have come by with questions and some trepidation. I believe in all of you. Over the next few weeks, we will laugh and we will cry and sometimes we will argue. And at those moments, we will discuss and process and continue to create."

At that moment I looked toward Erin. She had her eyes fixed on Mr. Bronson. Mia saw me looking and she looked over at Erin too. I then turned to Sullivan. He, too, was caught in a deep gaze on Mr. Bronson. I turned back to the center of the circle to listen more to Bronson.

"I have asked all the actors to be present today as well as our tech crew. I wanted all of you here today as we begin. So, where do we begin? I always like to start with making the story personal. As actors you will play characters that will have an entire range of emotions. How do you realistically play those strong emotions like anger or fear or disappointment? The characters in this musical do have a whole range of emotions that we need to capture and present to the audience, so it seems authentic to them. You will find that as you're acting, you may not feel the same point of view as your character. Something that would ignite a strong emotion out of the character may not light you up. We all have life experiences that have molded us to see the world around us a certain way. And those experiences allow us to react and respond to other situations. So today, I want to discuss how to tap into a strong emotion. How do you, as an actor, find a way to bubble that up and out? And then push it to the audience, so it feels real to them as we're trying to tell this story?"

Mr. Bronson stopped there and exited the circle. From the back of the room he announced to the group, "Create a group of two or three people. Group yourselves up in any way you want. If you're more comfortable with people you know, fine. Want to meet with people you don't know? Great." Bronson slid to the other side of the room. "Let's give ourselves one minute to create these small groups."

Quickly, chairs were pushed back and the cast began to pair themselves off. Many reached for those they knew. Very few were trying to venture out of their comfort zones, myself included. Mia grabbed my arm and I grabbed Erin's and we pushed our way to the back corner. Penny found herself with Sullivan and Allie. She looked over at us with a blank stare.

Mr. Bronson's booming voice began, "It looks like

we've gotten ourselves in groups of two and three. Well done."

Each group member was staring at Mr. Bronson waiting for direction.

"Think of one of the emotions that I discussed a few minutes ago. I mentioned anger, fear, and disappointment. I want you to think of a moment that taps into one of those feelings. Also, let's pair that with its opposite. So, the opposite of anger is, perhaps, indifference. The opposite of fear could be confidence or bravery. You can decide. And lastly, disappointment. A possible opposite may be joy or pride or fulfillment. Take some time to share a story in which you can pair both emotions. For example, you may share a story about fear of roller coasters. And you may go into detail about that time in you life when you felt pressured to ride the roller coaster but were absolutely terrified."

From the back, Jonah shouted, "Okay, Mr. B, tell us. What happened?"

The room was filled with laughter.

"A later date, thank you Jonah." Mr. Bronson smiled and continued his example. "And with this story of fear, you then share an unrelated moment in your life when you displayed confidence. Your partners don't need to feel that they must respond or give advice, unless you want it. This is a time just to listen."

The room buzzed with conversation as Mia, Erin,

and I looked at each other, as if to say, "Who wants to go first?"

Mia started. "I remember that moment when my parents sat me down and told me they were separating. This is my story of disappointment. Of course they did their best to break it to me gently, but it was so shocking to hear. I knew it had nothing to do with me, but in the end, I was the one left trying to figure out my new life. I guess they had to, too, but their choices caused a ripple effect for me. I'm used to it now and I'm much more aware of my parents as separate people and that they just wanted to be happy. And that's all I want. I want them to be happy. I need happiness, too."

Mia paused and took a deep breath. She looked around the room at the other cast members sharing stories.

"And I can pair that feeling of disappointment with confidence. I am hugely aware of my ability to take care of myself. I had to learn that, though. It was something inside of me that began to grow and develop when my parents split up. I know Mr. Bronson said that the emotions don't need to be connected, but I feel that in this case, they should or do."

Mia pulled her ponytail out and wrapped her hair band around her wrist. It's a habit she always does when she's falling deep into thought. "I guess that's it."

Erin began: "Fear." She looked at me and then at

Mia. "Fear of being left alone. I'm not talking about being home alone or being the last one to be picked up from school. I'm talking about not having anyone there for me. When my dad died, I became acutely aware and always in fear of losing my mom. What would happen to me if I lost her? Seriously, what happens? Losing my dad changed the foundation of my world as a safe place. Of course, I had plenty of reassurance and encouragement and I began to feel safe again. And it was at that moment that I was seeing and talking to my dad."

Mia and I just listened.

"Are you ready to hear my story?" Erin asked.

We nodded. I did a quick look around and the groups were still in full discussions. Mr. Bronson sat back at his desk watching all of us.

"My father was very sick. Once he was diagnosed, it seemed like he was gone within days. But in reality it was longer than that. I was holding on to every minute with him. I remember sitting in bed with him as he tried to read to me. His coughing and wheezing made it hard for him, so in return, I would read to him. We would read everything. He loved listening to me read aloud and he would ask my mom if I could stay up past my bedtime, just so we could read together. But one day he was so uncomfortable. It was very difficult for him to stay awake and be attentive. Our reading time ended, but I would sit outside his bedroom door and continue to read my books until I fell asleep on the floor. My mom would gather me up with my books and put me in my bed.

"On the night he died, I was asleep in my room. I heard voices in the house that I didn't recognize. I couldn't hear anything clearly, but I knew it was concerning my dad. I then heard movement in the hallway outside my bedroom door. When I slid out of my bed, the book I was reading hit the floor. I hoped no one would hear it and then come check on me. I sat there and didn't move. You should've seen how still I was. After a few minutes, I jumped down and went to my bedroom door. Carefully, I opened the door and peeked into the hallway just in time to watch the paramedics roll his hospital bed out of his room. But as I stood there watching this very dreamlike moment, I saw my dad standing with his back up against the wall with his finger to his mouth. He was making the *shhh* sign."

Listening to Erin's story, I found my skin began to bubble and tingle.

She continued, "I wasn't frightened or confused. I knew my dad was gone, but he was also right there."

I was reminded of my dad's story of when he saw his dad at the mailbox while walking Iggy.

Erin took a breath and then continued. "That was the first time of what I called 'shadowing.' I didn't have a name for it. I didn't know what to do with this at first. I would see him standing somewhere, like a shadow.

When I first mentioned it to my mom, she agreed that it was normal to grieve this way. But when I started communicating with him, I was so excited to share that with her. She still thought it was typical behavior of a child who has suffered a loss. When I continued to tell her that I was seeing him and talking to him, she nodded and it seemed like she believed me.

"I loved talking to him. And you have to believe me when I tell you that we spoke to each other. We didn't talk of what life was like after you died. We read books together. I shared what was happening at school. So I didn't see it to be a problem if I shared this with my friends at school. And because I was eleven years old, and at that age, you know, we were telling each other all kinds of stories, I sought out others to tell them that my dad was with me. And that we talk to each other.

"And that's when Sullivan came into my world. He was relentless. Not one day went by without a comment or a laugh. I remember meeting with the school counselor and she was very concerned about my well-being in the classroom. She would ask about my dad as if I was still grieving, but I wasn't. He was with me all the time. I kept looking for someone to listen to me, but it became very apparent that I just wasn't being heard. I could've easily listened to others' advice. I was being swallowed up by adults and their patronizing stories about how they grieved a loved one. I understand we all need to grieve. It may take on different forms, but it was clear to me that having my dad visit me was not what others wanted to hear.

"When the bullying became a daily occurrence and my shadowing was consistent, my mom made the decision to homeschool me. At first I was so sad, but to be honest, it gave me more time with my dad. Eventually the shadowing slowed down. I would go days without talking to my dad. But on some days, when he did visit me, I would see someone else walk by. I remember being distracted and looking over and past my dad to see someone standing there."

Mia and I looked at each other. Then back at Erin.

I asked, "Who?"

Erin shrugged. "I don't know, but it was someone."

"Wait, were you seeing other people other than your dad?" Mia asked.

"On a couple of visits with my dad, I would ask him who that was over there or who was the person sitting in the corner of the room or who was that person standing by the closet door?" Erin put her head down. "It was at that point my dad stopped visiting. It was as if he realized what was happening and by 'opening that door' others sought to find me too."

Mia asked, "When was the last time you were shadowing with your dad?"

Erin turned to look out the window and think.

"About a year ago." Erin's gaze returned to us. "I'm sad I don't visit with him the way I used to."

The three of us looked at each other. Erin said, "When my mom started dating your dad, Mia, it became really hard for me to feel like that channel that connected him to me could open anymore."

Mia reached for Erin's hand.

"And at this point, you know what happened next." Erin held Mia's hands. "And here we are."

"Here we are." I repeated.

With a big movement of papers and chairs, Mr. Bronson addressed the group. "Actors, thank you for sharing your stories. I'm so pleased to see and hear this group begin to gel and become one entity. We will continue with exercises like this in which you will be able to get to know one another."

The group began to shuffle around and find various spots in the room to sit, perch, or lean.

Erin turned back to us. "We never heard from you, Ty." Erin bit her bottom lip and furrowed her eyebrows as a way of saying, "I'm sorry I talked so much."

I put my hand up. "Both of your stories are way more interesting than anything I would have come up with. I was actually going to share a story of how I got lost at Disney World. It's not that interesting and it's hardly inspiring."

Mia took my hand and Erin laughed. Erin moved

from our small group and began to make her way to a chair. She was watching where Sullivan sat, maybe to avoid being right next to him.

While still holding my hand, Mia said, "You are very interesting, Ty Steiner."

I felt my stomach lurch.

11

"Today, I want to sing some songs." Bronson slid his way across the room. "I want us to create one voice. Many of you have listened and learned the music. I've heard many of you in the halls and in the cafeteria and out and around our school. If you have your scripts, turn to page eleven and look for the song titled 'Sit Down You're Rocking the Boat'."

Bronson pressed start on his laptop and the music began. The cast shuffled around to find a seat and turn to page eleven. I started singing as I already knew the song. Many actors began to sing. Mia and I stood next to each other searching and flipping pages for the song and lyrics in our scripts. Slowly, the collection of voices became one and we sang in unison. The group sounded great. We were beginning to start something new and create something that never existed before.

"Wonderful voices!" Mr. Bronson praised the cast. "Let's split ourselves up into small groups." Bronson gave his directions as the singing ended. "Find the partner to your character or the small group of people to your ensemble." Actors around the room began to move about to find each other. "Our dancers and our Havana singers, please find each other." The small groups began to form. "My tech crew, please join me here with your scripts as I want to give you some notes." Erin, Sullivan, and a couple of the other "techies" gathered to meet at the front of the room with Bronson.

"Here's the goal for the first ten minutes." Mr. Bronson began to pace the room. "Talk to the partner or small group about your character and what they're looking for. Discuss with the partners what you need as an actor to feel supported as you begin to create this character and develop their needs."

Allie and I met at the front door. With a heavy awkwardness, we stood there for a second and flipped through the pages of the script.

"We read this scene together already." Allie looked up. "At the audition."

"We did," I remarked. "We must've been good!"

Allie and I laughed a nervous laugh.

"I know you and Mia are really good friends and maybe this is weird because it's not her, but I want you to

know that this is just two characters…in their world…
in a different place." Allie stumbled over her words. "Are
you guys going out?"

I blinked.

"Um, well, um." I was completely caught off guard.

The room got quiet as Allie waited for a response.
When I took too long to answer, she started again.

"I get it," Allie continued. "I kinda heard Mia talking
to Penny, and I get it."

I wasn't sure what Allie was "getting." I looked over
to Mia and Matias running lines and giving each other
directions. Mia looked up at me at the same moment.
She smiled and widened her eyes. Mia pulled her hair
band off, fixed her hair and put the hair band back on.
She was thinking about something.

Allie began again. "I haven't given it too much
thought, but I really like this part of Adelaide. I like her
because she's funny and confident, and to be honest, she
has a big song that I know I can sing really well." Allie
shrugs. "What I need from you as an actor is to be able
to give me space when I need it, but work closely so the
comedy of Nathan and Adelaide seems authentic."

Apparently, this is Allie not giving it too much
thought.

"Okay. I can do all of that." I looked Allie in the eyes.
"You know, this is my first time in a school production,"
I tapped the script with my hand.

Allie nodded. "I know, so I was a bit surprised to see you on the cast list and even casted as Nathan."

Allie had no problem speaking her truth. This was something I didn't know about her.

"You did have a really good audition, and Mr. Bronson must think that you can pull this off."

Pull this off? I thought. The partnership of Nathan and Adelaide or Ty and Allie seemed to be starting off a bit rocky.

"Why don't we pick a spot to sit and read some lines?" I gestured to a corner by where we were standing.

As Allie turned around to walk to our spot, I caught Penny's glare. We both rolled our eyes. I wasn't sure what she was working through, but I figured we were both struggling with partners with healthy egos.

The afternoon wrapped up with a short motivational speech from Mr. Bronson. Mr. Bronson stood at the front of the room while the cast watched his every move. "Every little moment…every little breath can have a life of its own on stage. What I want you to think about while you're learning your lines or crafting a scene together with the other actors in this room is to understand that every scene must be split apart and rebuilt slowly through exploration and discovery. Each single moment that the audience watches and every muscle that each actor moves is a form of communication. That might be physical actions made by the actor."

Bronson swung his arms and did a little jig of a dance. The group laughed.

"Or bits of dialogue." Bronson grabbed a book sitting on his desk and held it up in the air as he spoke to it. "'Alas, poor Yorick! I knew him, Horatio.' It can even be the pauses on stage." Mr. Bronson softened his voice. "And even those moments of silence that bring some stillness to the stage"—Bronson froze and stared out the window. After a beat, he looked back at the group—"are absolutely essential and very important to the development of the characters and certainly the story. Think of this production like a Frankenstein monster. You're putting all the pieces of this new creature together. Begin to find ways to bring it to life. Sometimes, let others pump the blood. You don't always have to be the heart."

I looked toward Allie to see if she was listening. She was looking at her phone.

"We will be back tomorrow; full cast, please." Bronson held up his hand to indicate more information. "Please wear clothing to move in as we will begin some dancing and staging."

The room burst with excitement, part thrill of the production beginning and part relief that rehearsal was over for the day. I pulled my phone out of my backpack to see if my mom had texted me to say she was here or on her way. No messages from her. I moved toward Mia who looked like she was doing the same. Checking her phone. She looked up as I approached and smiled.

"My mom says she'll be here in five minutes. Let's wait outside." Mia grabbed my hand and we moved to the front door of the building and then waited outside for our parents.

Sullivan got up and shuffled his way through the crowd of excited actors to get to Erin. I watched as he talked to her with a sheepish look on his face. Her face seemed to soften as he spoke to her. She almost looked like she was smiling at him. I watched as a curious bystander. Mia slid in behind me.

"Allie is a lot," I remarked and looked over my shoulder. "She asked about us."

Mia looked over my shoulder, too. "Allie is a lot. But she is so wrapped up in herself that I wouldn't even worry about her," Mia said with disregard. "Can you come over to my house?"

"I haven't heard from my mom yet, but I'll text her and ask her if she can pick me up there." I reached into my pocket for my phone. Still no message from my mom. I sent a message telling her to meet me at Mia's. "Is it okay with your mom?"

"Ty, it's you." Mia smiled.

My phone buzzed with a quick response from my mom. I saw that my mom replied with a thumbs up emoji, a car, and the comedy and tragedy masks. I turned the phone so Mia could read her message. "I guess this means yes."

We heard a car honk its horn and saw that it was Michelle. Mia and I moved toward the direction of the parking lot to meet her. The car window slid down.

"Hi, guys!" Michelle was very excited. "How was your first rehearsal?"

Mia opened the door. "It was good. A lot of icebreakers and group activities. Jill is going to pick Ty up from our house, okay?"

"Of course, Ty. Please stay for dinner. Text your mom and ask if she wants to eat with us, too."

I opened the back door and slid in while I responded, "Thanks, Michelle. I'll ask."

The car ride home was a volley of inquisitive questions and brief responses between Mia and Michelle. I injected my thoughts and opinions when I felt it was appropriate.

"My mom said she'll pick me up later and thank you for dinner, but she already ate."

The car trip to Mia's house was quick and before I knew it we were pulling up to her house. Quickly, Mia jumped out and opened my door. I gathered my backpack and phone and followed her into the garage and into the house.

Mia called back to Michelle, "We're going to begin to run lines and work on some homework. Do you need us to help with dinner?"

Michelle responded, "No, thank you. It'll be ready in about twenty minutes."

Mia and I walked down the hallway that led to the stairs. I scratched the top of Missy's head. We slipped into Mia's room. I dropped my backpack on the floor of her room. I had been in her bedroom millions of times, but now it felt different. I slid myself into her desk chair and swiveled around. Mia kicked off her sneakers and fell into an overstuffed bean bag. We stared at each other. I got up from the chair and placed both knees on the bean bag. I teetered over so we were now both looking at each other, face to face. Mia and I moved in to kiss.

"I didn't say anything to Allie when she asked about you and me," I explained myself. "All she said was that she heard you and Penny talking and she knows that we're friends, but she thought that because our characters in the play are dating that it would be awkward." I rambled, and Mia kissed my nose.

"I told Penny about us." Mia's response didn't quite match my story, but I could see where she was going. "Penny was shocked at first, but then she had a slightly jealous tone, although I think she's really into Cali Denton."

I took Mia's hand. "This is all new to me, so I don't even know how to respond to people. I'm not afraid of what people's response will be, I just know that we haven't really talked about it."

Mia's thumb rolled over my hand. "Well, we like each other and we've spent some time kissing. And we were always together anyway, so the response seems easy." Mia kissed me again.

"Should we check on your mom and see if she needs help?" I offered, although I slid deeper into the beanbag.

Mia crinkled her nose and nodded. I rolled out of the bean bag and stood up. I pulled at Mia's hands and lifted her up and turned her to the door. With her shoulders slacked, she and I headed toward the kitchen.

After dinner, Mia and I offered to clean up the kitchen. Glasses and plates and bowls of food were scattered across the table and on the kitchen counter. The image of an enjoyable meal. Michelle was so grateful as she pulled out her phone to respond to some of her text messages.

"Thank you for dinner." Mia hugged her mom.

I watched the interchange between Mia and her mom. Michelle put down her phone and then pulled a strand of Mia's hair that was covering her eye and placed it behind Mia's ear. Mia picked up Michelle's phone, opened the camera up, and turned it around to take a picture of the two of them. They look so much alike. Mia turned and placed a kiss on her mother's cheek as she took a second picture. Michelle giggled. Mia handed the phone back to Michelle.

"Can you take a picture of Ty and me?" Mia moved

next to me by the sink with all the dishes piled up and slid her arm around my waist.

While Michelle adjusted the camera, Mia whispered, "Our first photo." Mia and I moved in closer to each other and Michelle captured the moment.

We have millions of pictures of us together through the years. There is one I always think about. We were at a birthday party and we both had our mouths filled with cake. Someone caught us eating and laughing at the same time. It's a great picture, but this one is the first photo of "us."

We finished cleaning up the kitchen when my phone buzzed with a text from my mom telling me she was five minutes away. The text also included a kissing face, a stoplight, and a car. I shook my head and smiled.

"My mom is almost here. I should get my stuff from your room," I announced.

Mia and I moved through the kitchen and back to her room. I bent down to pick up my backpack when I noticed that the script we were going to run lines with was sitting there, unmoved. I slid the backpack onto my shoulder and moved in close to Mia.

"This was fun. I had fun tonight." We placed our foreheads on each other. I got a glimpse outside Mia's window and saw that my mom had pulled up to the house. Immediately, my phone buzzed. I swiped open the phone and texted:

OMW

Mia and I hugged once more and I turned to head out of her bedroom.

"Bye, Michelle. My mom is here. Thank you for dinner," I yelled into the house.

Michelle moved from the kitchen and into the front hallway. "Bye, Ty." She smiled. "Anytime." She winked. Missy stood by her side.

Mia tilted her head up and kissed me. Does Michelle know? Well, she does now. I pulled back with widened eyes. Mia winked too. I opened the front door and noticed that I skipped for a second as I headed to my mom's car. Mom waved to me from the car.

12

In the cafeteria the next day, our new group found its way to a larger table. We pulled up chairs and dropped our lunches on the table. Some of us switched items from the bags for something better. Immediately, we all compared stories of our experiences at rehearsal the day before.

Mia entertained the group with a funny story about her first play with Mr. Bronson. Penny brought Cali to the table, and they both laughed with Mia. Erin launched into questions about what it would be like behind the scenes, and Sullivan echoed her concerns. Each of us gave some advice. Our banter overlapped with each other, laughing at our exaggerated stories, our hands and arms gesturing for the comedy and stuffing our faces with each other's food. The hum of the cafeteria became the soundtrack to our little scene in the cafeteria. I reached under the table and held Mia's hand. She squeezed back.

Sullivan held his hand up to ask for the group's attention. "Can I say something?"

We paused as Sullivan composed himself. He took a moment to swallow the food in his mouth. Erin looked down at the table and then looked out across the cafeteria.

"I feel really comfortable here. I feel like all of you could have pushed me away or made it known that I wasn't welcome." Sullivan scratched his head. "I'm working on being a different person. A better person." He tilted his head at the word "better." "This is going to take me some time, but none of you have asked me for anything, and that makes me feel like I'm capable of change." Sullivan turned toward Erin. "Erin, I am so sorry. I am so sorry for everything I ever said or did that made you feel hurt."

At this point Penny started crying. Cali put her arm around her.

"I really want you to know that." Sullivan smiled.

Erin reached across the table and took Sullivan's hands. I looked at Mia and then back at Erin.

Erin said, "You really know how to kill a vibe, Sully."

Some of us laughed at Erin's comment. Erin called him "Sully." Using that nickname did two things. First, it told Sullivan that she accepted his apology and second, it gave her the upper hand. No one called Sullivan "Sully" other than his mom and, I think, his brother. Sullivan lifted his head up and smiled.

"Sullivan, I'm trying, as well, to navigate this too, and I appreciate the space you're giving me to move into this life again."

Penny was now full-on sobbing. Cali was reaching for napkins.

"I see that you're working on becoming the person you want to be. I am, too. Let's agree that this is the beginning of a new beginning. We'll try to support each other as we grow. Can we agree to that? Can we agree that this is not a quick fix, but a slow and steady change for the better?"

Sullivan nodded his head. "Bronson wants to meet with the tech crew before rehearsal today. Will you be there?"

Sullivan nodded his head again.

"Good." Erin brought her hands back. "I need someone there to explain to me what's happening. I literally have no idea."

Sullivan smiled and gave a smug look, proud that he was being called upon to help in a crisis.

Penny pulled back her curly hair, took a hearty sniff, and wiped her eyes on a napkin that Cali gave her. "Okay, I'm done. This lunch was too much. You guys are too much." Another sniff and blow into the napkin. "Sullivan, I'm so happy that you're making some changes.

Erin, I'm so happy to have you back in my life again. You are so chill and cool. And Cali and I are going out, and so are Mia and Ty."

Mia and I smiled at Penny while she gave her speech. "Can we put it out there? Are we all good?" Classic Penny.

She continued. "But I'd made a pact to myself that I would never cry in the school cafeteria."

The group of us laughed.

"Go ahead and laugh, but I'm back at zero days again since I last cried and it's all because of you people."

We laughed again.

Mia asked, "What day were you on?"

Penny replied, "I was only at eight, but I was trying to get to ten."

Our laughter wasn't about teasing Penny; it was about her comedic timing. Penny began to laugh as well.

Cali opened up the rehearsal schedule on her phone. "We're working on the opening scene this afternoon and some of us may be pulled to practice our songs."

We nodded at her information.

"I know the dancers will be in the opening number," Cali continued.

The bell rang to begin the dismissal of the lunch period and get us moving toward our next class. All of us grabbed our trash and cups and lunch bags and moved toward the garbage cans. We then all slipped out the cafeteria doors.

I took Mia's hand. We moved ahead of the group through the hallway.

"Sullivan is really working on making a change and it seems like Erin's okay with it," Mia remarked.

"I know. I can see that he is legitimately committed to correcting things with Erin," I responded. "I wonder what the motivation was for him?"

The hallway was too loud and crowded for us to have a serious conversation about the newest "new" developments. Or to discuss Sullivan's father's current health. As we passed through the congested hallway, I thought about my mom's comment again: "Try something new." I also thought about the Maya Angelou poem Mr. Atkin assigned us to read. I reminded myself about the one line that says, "Nobody can make it out here alone."

Does the universe put things out there for us to put together like a puzzle? Do these sound bites and snippets build upon one anther to show you a way and give you a sense of stability and hope and promise? Do I have to look for them or do they come to me? Do I have to be aware of it to capture them to learn from it? As I wondered, I felt Mia's hand squeeze mine as she stopped walking.

"I'm going in there." Mia lifted her chin to point. "Meet me here when the bell rings and we can walk to Bronson's room."

"Okay." I reached for a hug.

As we pulled apart she waved. I continued to walk

down the crowded hallway, foggy in thought.

At the end of class, I gathered my books and slid them into my backpack. I pulled myself up from the desk and made my way out of class. I felt energized even though today at lunch may have looked like a sad group of kids huddled around a table. And at that table some were crying, some were spilling their emotional guts, and some were looking and listening with open eyes and attentive ears. For me, it was a moment that I felt the closest to a group of people. I gently made my way out of the classroom to meet Mia.

The opening scene of the production had all of us on stage. Mr. Bronson arranged us in groups of three or four and showed us how to walk across the stage. Each group crossed the others to the beat of the music. We were to react to the scene of a bustling New York City corner. Each one of us was in character.

13

"Group one, please move to stage left. Group four, when group one moves, you move across." Mr. Bronson was directing the actors on how to walk across the stage during the opening scene. "Stay in character. Remember who you are."

As the groups slid back and forth across the stage, Sam, who played Nicely-Nicely, moved to center stage and began to sing the song, "I've Got the Horse." He sounded great. I found myself listening and not in character.

Mr. Bronson noticed, too. "Ty, stay in character please. Interact with Adelaide, please."

Allie looked annoyed.

I moved back to my spot on stage and had an improvised and silent conversation with her. The song ended and Mr. Bronson gave us a mediocre round of applause.

"Okay. Can I see the tech crew to give some notes on how this will look on stage?"

Sullivan and Erin got up from their chairs and moved closer to Mr. Bronson. I was aware by their body language that things didn't seem as strained between them. I thought I saw Erin actually smile at Sullivan. The actors on stage moved to spots to sit, wrote some notes in their scripts, and ran some lines. Allie and I did the same. We found a corner and pulled up two chairs and decided to look at a scene that had the potential to be a disaster—solely by me, if I'm honest.

Rehearsal ended on a really high note. Allie and I performed a scene together that had the actors laughing and applauding.

Allie turned to me at the end of the scene. "That was great!"

A compliment from Allie Mussard.

Mr. Bronson was smiling and announced, "And this is why I casted you two in these roles!" He continued the applause. I scanned the room to see everyone smiling or clapping or giving a thumbs up.

"My cast, we have come to the end of today's rehearsal. Plan on being here tomorrow to work with the band." The room murmured with excitement. "We'll just be singing the songs so please be aware of your lines and the lyrics," Mr. Bronson continued to explain. "Tomorrow is what is called a *sitzprobe*. It's a funny word, but in musical theater a sitzprobe is a rehearsal where the singers sing with the orchestra. We are focusing our attention on integrating or fusing the two groups. This will be the first rehearsal of many where the orchestra and singers rehearse and perform together. We do this so the actors sing the songs while the band performs, and the groups begin to feel comfortable with each other."

We were all in rapt attention as Mr. Bronson spoke. He then nodded to indicate he was finished speaking, and that we could now begin to gather our stuff and get ready to leave.

Mr. Bronson raised his hand.

"One last thing. Please be aware that tomorrow's rehearsal may run a little later than usual, so plan for your 'pickups' and your carpooling today."

I walked over to Mia.

"Ty, that scene with you and Allie was so funny!" She grabbed my hand and squeezed it.

I felt myself blush.

"I have to admit, Allie is a really good actor." I nodded.

"She is, but you two are so funny together."

Mia and I began to walk out of Mr. Bronson's drama room. I noticed that our little group had gathered around together by the lockers. Cali, Penny, Erin, and Sullivan turned to Mia and to me as we approached the group.

"My brother can drive us to get something to eat," Sullivan announced.

We were all on a high from a great rehearsal, and it was obvious he wanted to ride the wave and go get something to eat with his new group of friends.

"My mom is almost here," Penny said, pointing to her phone. "And we're driving Cali home."

"My mom is on her way, too." Erin answered.

Sullivan thought for a second and said, "Okay. Tomorrow. Bronson says tomorrow's rehearsal will run late. We can get something to eat after rehearsal. Ben won't mind driving us."

"Your brother can't fit us all in his car," I pointed out.

"Why don't we all just meet there?" Mia asked. "My mom can take the four of us and Ben can drive you."

"Will your mom mind driving us and then picking us up after we eat?" Penny asked.

Mia pulled her hair band off. "We live so close to school. She won't mind."

I offered the next suggestion. "I can ask my mom or dad to pick us up, so your mom doesn't have to drive both ways."

Sullivan smiled because his idea of a dinner with his new group of friends was taking shape. Our phones began to buzz with text messages from the people who were picking us up. We all sent our messages that we were walking out of the building and ready to go home. Sullivan moved closer to Erin and smiled. Erin smiled back with a cautious grin. Sullivan said something to her. They high-fived each other. Erin kind of smiled with a bit of an eye roll. She turned to head for the exit of the hallway.

Mia said to Erin, "Our parents are here."

Erin and Mia began to walk ahead. Penny and Cali were looking and laughing at something on Cali's phone and then they began to walk away.

Sullivan stopped me before I walked away. "Steiner, can I ask you something?"

"Sure," I answered.

Sullivan stared at me.

The hallway began to quiet as the cast members moved down to the exit. Sullivan continued to stare at me.

"Are you okay?" I was reminded of what had happened a few days ago, when I found him in the building alone.

"Do you think Erin is feeling better about things with me? I feel like she is." Sullivan, whose voice is usually booming, was surprisingly soft. I gathered my thoughts for a second.

"Well, I have noticed that she seems to be more relaxed with you and being back in school again." I wasn't sure what Sullivan wanted me to say.

"I know this is weird and with our history, but

spending time with Erin while we're teching the play…I feel like we've gotten closer." Sullivan looked right at me. And I knew where this conversation was going.

"I think I understand." I turned back to see Mia waiting at the exit and I held up my finger to tell her to wait. She nodded.

I turned back to Sullivan. "Erin said that she wants to move very cautiously and slowly into school and make new friends, so… if you're asking me what I think you're asking me, my advice is just take it slow and let things work themselves out. And if it's meant to be, you'll know."

I hoped I was giving Sullivan what he needed while also looking out for Erin. Sullivan smiled and nodded. That was a good sign. He and I walked down the long hallway in silence. I could sense from him that he was satisfied with my answer because he was smiling and swinging his arms a bit. Mia watched us as Sullivan and I marched in unison.

Sullivan waved to us both and walked out the glass door to meet his brother outside.

"Erin is in the car already, but I wanted to say 'bye '." Mia hugged me.

While in our hug, I whispered, "I think Sullivan likes Erin."

Mia pulled back and stared at me.

I shrugged. "I know. He just told me. Well, he told me in his own Sullivan way." I shrugged again.

Mia moved to my side, so we could walk together. "Okay. Wow. Does Erin know this?"

I noticed Erin in the back of Mia's dad's car. Talia was sitting up front.

"I don't know," I answered. "Sullivan made it sound like they've been getting close during the rehearsals," I explained.

"I'm thinking that maybe you shouldn't say anything to Erin." Mia approached the car door, nodded her head, hugged me, and then got into her car. Surprisingly, the hair band stayed in.

"Very interesting," she whispered as she slid in the backseat.

I waved to all the members of the car and looked out over the parking lot to see my mom's car waiting for me. My mom waved as I walked to her car.

I tossed my backpack onto the backseat of the car and jumped in the front. My mom was staring at me with big eyes and a wide grin.

"What?" I snapped. "Sorry, that came out harsh, but why are you looking at me that way?"

She tilted her head. She cupped her hands and fingers around the steering wheel and moved them around the wheel. Each hand created a half moon shape. She looked out the front window and then looked back at me.

I laughed. "What?"

"You were just walking hand in hand with Mia, and

then there was a passionate hug. That's what," she began her interrogation. "I knew it. I knew it!"

I dropped my head. "Passionate? Can we go home?"

My mom laughed out loud again. Her laugh was more of a silly giggle. She began to move the car through the parking lot of the school.

"All I'm saying is, I knew it." She laughed. "Can I ask you any questions?" She turned her head to me and then back out the window and then back at me.

I mumbled, "It depends."

"What?" she asked.

"It depends," I repeated clearly.

"It depends? What does that mean?" She giggled. "I just have something to ask."

My head was now resting on the window. "Okay."

"My first question," she began.

"Wait, your first question?" I turned back to her.

"Ty, very funny. This is very exciting!" She was trying to keep her eyes on the road as she began to interrogate me.

"This is very embarrassing." I went back to mumbling again.

As we drove home, my mom asked me questions like "How long?," "How did this start?," and "Who else knows?" It was her way of asking if my dad knew yet or if she was the first to know.

I gave her honest answers without giving away too

much. I tried to have some privacy without being private. And to be truthful, this was all very new, so I really didn't have much to say other than that Mia and I were happy being together.

"Well, I'm very happy for both of you. You've been friends for so long, that the whole 'getting to know you' awkward stage won't be a thing."

I nodded from my seat and caught her smiling again. I needed a change of subject, so I mentioned that tomorrow after rehearsal, some of us were going to get something to eat.

"Mia was going to ask her mom if she could drive us to the restaurant and maybe you or Dad could pick us up?" I asked.

"Of course, just let us know where and when. I'll speak to Michelle, too." She drove the car up to our house and into the driveway.

I could see Iggy from the front window. His tail was wagging with excitement. I reached for my backpack in the backseat and jumped out of the car.

"Wait, Ty," my mom called for me. I bent down to look back into the car. "Before we go in and get Iggy all excited and begin to make dinner, I want to tell you that I am very proud of the person you are and the person you are becoming." She blinked slowly. "I don't want you to ever think for one second that I'm not impressed with the way you've handled a life that was given to you."

I placed my backpack down on the driveway and got back into the car. "Thank you?" I said with a question mark in my response. "I'm very happy, Mom."

We both sat in silence for a second, when I said, "Sometimes things just suck, but I know that I have you and Dad here with me, to make things kinda suck…less."

My brain did a quick montage of images showing me what Erin's days must have been like when her father died, as well as what Sullivan must have been going through as his father dealt with his own illness and recovery.

"I know you have your friends now to listen to you and that's wonderful. They should be there for you, but I want you to know that Dad and I will always be here, too."

"I know." I turned to Iggy's barks coming from the house. "Iggy is about to lose it."

Mom finished with, "I love you."

"I love you, too." I hopped out of the car and closed the car door to go to Iggy's rescue, but then stopped, turned around, and bent back into the window to smile at my mom.

She smiled back.

Erin's Journal

My days at school are getting better. I like having a schedule outside of my mom creating that schedule for me. Today, Mia told me Sullivan asked if I was feeling better about things with him. He said he feels like we've gotten closer. Closer. I don't even know how to process that word when it comes to him. It's like he's trying to make up for everything he put me through, but it's more than just guilt. I can see it in the way he looks at me—there's something genuine there. I can't lie. I've caught myself looking at him, too. He's got this crooked smile that's kind of…sweet? And when he talks about the lighting or the set design or ways to improve the flow of actors on stage or cracks a joke about the chaos backstage, I feel something shift. I can't tell if it's forgiveness, friendship, or something more. I was very lonely so I don't want to trick myself into thinking more than what this is.

Sullivan is now going through something too. He is making his way into people's lives that haven't wanted him there in a long time. If anyone can appreciate that, hell, I sure can! But I'm not ready for anything more. Not yet. I've spent so long trying to rebuild myself, to let go of those awful memories, and I'm scared to trust him fully. What if he doesn't mean it? What if this is just some game for him, and I end up hurt all over again? Still, part of me hopes. Maybe people can change. Maybe we can leave the past behind and build something new. Mia says to take it slow, and that's probably the best advice I could get. For now, I'll focus on the play, on school, and on figuring out how I fit back in. But for the first time in years, I'm not scared of him. And that, in itself, feels like a victory.

14

The cast arrived in Mr. Bronson's classroom at a slow and steady pace. I found a spot in the room to place my backpack and waited for Mia and the rest of the group. I seemed to always be the first to arrive. Mia came rushing into the room and grabbed me.

"Erin went to her locker," she said, out of breath.

"Okay," I responded.

Mia looked around the room and then dragged me by my arm to a far corner of Mr. Bronson's classroom. "I was just talking to Erin about the play and school and being a little stressed out about everything when she said…" Mia pulled at her hair band, but didn't take it out.

I looked straight at Mia, waiting for some information.

She continued, "When she said, 'Sullivan seems to be trying to be my friend'."

I guess I didn't react the way Mia would have liked, so she pulled my arm.

"Ty, she asked me if I think it's okay for her to be friends with Sullivan. And after what you told me yesterday, don't you think that's interesting?"

More students entered the room and the level of noise due to the voices increased. The musicians, who would be playing along, began to set up their instruments and a crescendo of honking horns, beating drums, and the strumming of guitars filled the room.

"I guess," I replied over the din. It seemed like I still wasn't giving Mia the reaction she was looking for.

"All I'm saying is that in the quick conversation I had with Erin on the way here, I think she likes him," Mia said coyly.

Her smug smile made me laugh out loud.

"I'm telling you, Ty, watch them today during rehearsal and tell me otherwise."

Mia squeezed my hand and turned to find a place to sit. She waved to Penny and Cali, who had walked in together. Erin followed behind. Sullivan came running in shortly after, looking startled and a bit bewildered. He caught my eye and gave me a thumbs up. Sullivan moved closer to me. He was somewhere between running and walking very purposefully.

"Steiner!" Sullivan called to me in a whisper shout. "Can I talk to you?" Sullivan waved me over to where he had stopped running.

I turned to Mia. "I'll be right back."

I dropped my script on my chair and moved to Sullivan. He had a smile across his face.

"What's the matter? Are you okay?" I asked him.

Sullivan looked over my shoulder. I turned around to see Erin, Penny, and Cali gathering chairs together and making a small grouping. They began to sit down. Erin looked up at me, smiled, and shook her head.

"Sullivan?" I pressed.

"Erin is really cool. I mean she is like, *really* cool." Sullivan smiled wider.

"Okay, what happened between when the bell rang and now?" I continued. "You talked to her about something?"

"I did. I saw her at her locker and I asked if I could tell her something." Sullivan looked down at his hands. "I told her that my dad may be sick again." Sullivan looked up. "I asked her if she and I could meet somewhere this weekend so maybe she could kinda tell me what to say and do." Sullivan smiled.

I smiled. "That's great, Sullivan." I corrected myself. "No, not great. What I mean is, I'm glad you're both working this out."

Sullivan nodded. He knew what I meant. "I really like her, Steiner. I think she likes me *back*." Sullivan said the word "back" with a questioning intonation.

I wanted to give Sullivan my full attention, but I could sense that Bronson was starting as the room was getting quiet.

Sullivan finished with, "We're all still going out tonight, right?"

"Yes," I assured him. "Tonight'll be fun. You and Erin can continue where you left off at the lockers."

Sullivan blushed. "Erin hugged me."

"What!?" I barked out louder than I expected. "Sorry. That's great." I whispered. "Sorry, I keep saying *great*."

"Let's find our seats, please," Mr. Bronson announced.

Sullivan slipped off before I had a chance to ask any more questions. I stood for a second and turned to go back to my seat.

"As you see and hear, we have the band here today. So, I want to be respectful of everyone's time."

The voices and instruments began to quiet as Mr. Bronson continued his direction for the day's rehearsal. I walked back to my seat.

"A quick reminder that today's sitzprobe will start at the top of the show, but we may need to stop and tighten something up, give the band and the actors some time to find each other in the songs." He moved about the room. "I ask that you all pay close attention to where you need to be and be prepared to sing. I'm not interested in catching anyone up and showing them where they need to be."

Mr. Bronson could be firm, but it earned the cast's respect.

I saw that Mr. Bronson had placed some X's on the floor with green tape near the band. It seemed to be a mark to give the actors a designated place to stand for when they'd be singing along.

He continued, "Many of the scenes have multiple singers, so you may stand at your seat if needed, rather than coming up to these designated spots." He pointed to the X's.

The cast shuffled in their seats and pulled out scripts, put away phones, and moved closer to cast members they might be singing with. Allie found a spot near me.

"Okay, *Guys and Dolls*. Let's begin at the top of the show!" Mr. Bronson made one of his big arm movements as if to start our engines.

Actors continued to stand and find a spot to sing. The band began with the opening number and the sitzprobe began.

"Steiner." Sullivan, who was sitting behind me, leaned over my shoulder. I could see he had a pencil tucked behind one ear and the green highlighter placed on top of the other ear. "Think about where we can eat after rehearsal."

He gave me another thumbs up, and I nodded and whispered, "Okay."

I noticed that Erin was sitting next to him writing

notes in her script. Turning back around to scan the room, I looked for Mia. She was sitting across the room with Matias. We caught each other's eyes and she smiled a "told you so" smile. Oh, she didn't know the latest!

Throughout the rehearsal I observed Erin and Sullivan comparing notes, leaning into each other to whisper something or laugh at something that struck them as funny. Sullivan pulled up something on his phone that made her laugh. It was the first time I'd seen Erin totally relaxed since I'd met her.

Allie and some of the ensemble ended the sitzprobe with an amazing performance. I kept telling myself that even though Allie required me to give her space on stage to allow her character to grow, which is something she'd remind me of often, I had to admit she *was* really good.

The cast applauded each other for a successful rehearsal. Mr. Bronson was shaking his head and smiling. That had to be a good sign. It was at that moment that I came to the realization that being a part of this production was really important. In my head, I was trying to think of a tree pun. Had I shown some *growth*? Nah. I was *stumped*. Ugh. Where was Mia?

The cast continued to fill the room with energy that seemed electric. It was clear to us that this production was special. I looked around and saw everyone laughing and smiling. I caught Sullivan and Erin sitting together comparing notes on their scripts. They were still laughing!

Mia came from behind me. I turned around to catch her gaze. "You sounded so good." I gave her a tight hug.

Penny walked over to us. "This was great and all, but I'm starving."

"Me too," Mia agreed. "Where's Sullivan?"

"He asked me to think of some places to go eat. How about we meet at Puff Burgers?" Penny suggested. "They have great milkshakes and their spicy fries are so good."

We all agreed that Puff Burgers was the place to go. Mia texted her mom to see if she was here and could take us there. Penny left to go get Cali, and I walked over to Sullivan and Erin. Erin was putting away her script and gathering her army green sack. When I approached, I heard Sullivan ask her a question.

"Can't you just come with Ben and me?" Sullivan pleaded.

"I'm gonna ride with Mia, Sullivan," she said firmly. "We can all meet there." She flung her sack over her shoulder.

"It's going to be crowded in her car with all of you," Sullivan pushed, not wanting to take no for an answer.

"Mia's mom has a van," I said.

Erin and Sullivan looked toward me.

Sullivan conceded with a nod of agreement. "Okay, but next time. And also I'm getting my license soon. I'm getting it in March," he announced. "I'll be able to drive all of us!"

The classroom of actors began a slow descent into quiet. The band members had packed up their instruments and many of the cast members had left. Some were slowly exiting as their phones lit up with a parent announcing they were here for pick up.

Mia, Erin, Penny, Cali, and I stood at the front door waiting for Mia's mom to pick us up. Sullivan approached us with a huge grin.

"Ben's almost here. Are you sure you don't want to split up and ride with us?"

Mia stepped in this time to shield Erin. "Sullivan, I've seen your brother's car. Ben's car can only hold the two of you."

"Someone can sit in the back," Sullivan pointed out. "I'll sit in the back," he offered.

Mia's phone lit up at that moment. "My mom is here. We'll all meet at Puff Burgers."

The group of us headed to Mia's mom's minivan. I hadn't thought about the fact that Erin, Mia's dad's girlfriend's daughter, was now being picked up and driven by Mia's mom. No one seemed to be reacting, so I certainly wasn't going to mention anything.

"Don't be bummed out," I whispered to Sullivan on the way out. "This is all good. We'll meet at the restaurant."

The girls walked ahead of me toward the van.

Sullivan nodded. "Ben's almost here."

I reached over and slapped Sullivan on the shoulder.

"Order me a cookies-and-cream milkshake," he called out. It was my turn to give a thumbs up.

Mia asked me, "Do you want to sit up front and I can get in the back?"

She had already made the decision to do so as she climbed first into the van. Erin moved in next, followed by Cali and Penny. I jumped in the front seat and Michelle greeted me with a big smile.

"Okay, we're going to Puff Burgers. Everyone buckled in?" Michelle directed the group.

The car pulled away from school while Sullivan stood on the sidewalk waiting for his brother to arrive.

"Sullivan really wanted you to go with him, Erin." Penny launched into the hot topic right away.

I turned my head over my left shoulder to watch the interaction and conversation.

Erin pulled her green sack up on her lap. "Sullivan is really trying." Erin looked right at Penny. "I can't help but notice that."

Penny continued, "Are you feeling better about him?" Penny's voice softened.

The van was quiet. Michelle continued to keep a watchful eye on the road while peeking into the rearview mirror to catch some quick images of Erin's reactions.

"You would think that I'd be pushing him away, right? You would think that out of all the people in our school, Sullivan would be the last person I would be working with so closely. But he's being very nice and honest and…" Erin trailed off. "I have to let the past be the past. If I don't do that, I can't heal either."

I heard sniffling and this time it wasn't Penny. I caught Michelle wiping her eyes. She looked toward me and shook her head.

Penny reached over to take Erin's hand. "You really are a cool person, Erin. I'm glad we're back in each other's lives again." Erin took Penny's hand and squeezed. The car ride remained quiet for some time. We sat and looked at our phones, stared out the windows or closed our eyes. Erin reached into her green sack and pulled out her journal and pen. By the light of the passing street lights, Erin wrote in her journal.

Erin's Journal

Penny's words stuck with me. "Are you feeling better about him?" It's such a simple question, but answering it made me realize how much I've been holding on to. How much I've let the past define me as a person. My history is my history and not anyone else's. I know what I can endure. A lot! I'm not the "ghost girl" anymore.

Sullivan surprised me. Of all people, I never thought he'd be the one to show me kindness, honesty, and understanding. I used to see him as part of the problem, a reminder of things I wanted to forget. But now, I'm starting to see that maybe people can change or maybe I can.

I said it out loud and I will write it here. I have to let the past be the past. It's like the words unlocked something in me, a small but important step toward healing. Penny took my hand. I'm not alone. There are people who see the good in me even when I struggle to see it in myself.

I caught Michelle wiping her eyes. Even her life was turned upside down too, and she is driving me around. She's very confident in herself to have the daughter of the woman who is dating her former husband in her van. I mean, what is this life?

The silence in the car wasn't awkward; it was peaceful. A kind of stillness I needed to absorb everything. I don't know where this "road" leads, but for the first time in a while, I feel like I'm moving forward. Oh, and to Puff Burgers.

Michelle broke the silence, "Do you all have rehearsal tomorrow?"

"Some of us do—the dancers and the main characters. Tech crew is also called." Mia scrolled her phone to look at the rehearsal schedule Mr. Bronson posted.

Michelle nodded her head. I noticed Puff Burgers on the right. Michelle brought the car into the parking lot and drove us right up to the front door. We reached for our belongings and hopped out of the minivan.

"Mia, text me when you're ready to be picked up," Michelle called out.

"My dad may be able to get us, Michelle," I replied.

"Okay, just text me and keep me posted."

The group of us thanked Mia's mom for driving us and waved as she pulled away from the restaurant.

Puff Burgers was a neon-soaked restaurant. Every wall had some bright neon message emblazoned to it. Messages like, "Burgers are gold, but you are golden." or "Puff Burgers make things hot!" or "Fries or lies, you choose!" as well as "Take your hips and shake 'em!"

Mia led the group of us to a large table toward the back of the restaurant. We pulled out our chairs and all flopped into them. An audible sigh was heard from all of us.

"I haven't been here in years," Cali remarked. "I feel like I had my eleventh birthday party here."

On the table was a plastic holder with a list of all the milkshakes that Puff Burgers offers. I scanned the list looking for cookies-and-cream for Sullivan and I noticed a chocolate peanut butter milkshake for me.

Mia leaned into me not to say anything, just to relax her body against mine. She looked at the milkshake menu, too, and announced, "Strawberry marshmallow looks so good!"

The waitress arrived to take our order, dressed in a

neon retro uniform to look like she was a waitress from the 1950s. She wore a hot pink apron and her name tag said "Francesca."

"Hi guys, welcome to Puff Burgers." She pulled out her notepad and scanned the table. She quickly noticed that Erin was wearing a black Nirvana t-shirt. "Okay, girl, I gotta ask," Francesca smirked looking toward Erin. "Can you name two Nirvana songs?"

Erin looked up from the menu and with a smug tone said, "Only two?" She threw her hands up. "We can start with 'Smells Like Teen Spirit,' just because, but let's add 'Sliver' and 'Come As You Are,' 'Heart-Shaped Box' and my favorite, 'Lithium'." Erin elegantly interlaced her fingers together and slowly placed them on the table and then closed her eyes.

Francesca snapped her notepad shut and began to clap her hands. "Well done, girl!"

Erin laughed. "In Kurt we Trust."

Francesca repeated, "Oh yes, In Kurt we Trust."

The group of us smiled toward Francesca as a sign that we were ready to place our orders.

We each took our turn giving our burger and milkshake orders. Mia, strawberry marshmallow. Penny, pina colada. Cali, blueberry cheesecake. And Erin, mocha malt. After everyone else had ordered, I ordered mine and I made sure to order Sullivan's milkshake, too.

"We have someone else coming. He'll be here any

minute. Cookies-and-cream is for him," I explained.

"Oh my friend, one person ordering two milkshakes is not unusual," our waitress remarked. "We don't judge at Puff Burgers."

Before Francesca walked away, Penny asked for a large order of the spicy fries for the table and plenty of napkins.

On the wall was a cat clock, the type where its eyes and tail move to the mark of each second. I looked at the clock and then at the front door. Sullivan should have been here by now. Ben either forgot or was running late to pick him up. The table spent time discussing the rehearsals, complaining about homework, talking about people we knew, and going over what our plans would be once the play was over.

Francesca returned to the table with a second waitress. The two waitresses were carrying trays and balancing all the milkshakes and the big basket of spicy fries. We helped them by moving around the plates and silverware to make room for our food and drinks. The waitresses called out each order and we reached for the big glass mugs as our milkshakes were announced. I took Sullivan's and placed it near me. I looked back at the cat clock and the door.

Penny took a long slurp of her milkshake and cried, "Brain freeze!"

Cali almost spit out her big sip of milkshake as Penny

over exaggerated a motion of bringing her hand to her head. Mia and I reached for the fries as Erin pulled out the straw from her glass mug and let the milkshake drip off the straw and into her mouth. Erin let the straw continue to drip. At the last drop, she grabbed a napkin and tried to sound nonchalant as she made an announcement. "Sullivan wants to go out this weekend."

She looked at the faces around the table. Penny was visibly shocked. Wide eyes and mouth agape. "Excuse me?" she blurted. "I'm sorry. Go out?"

"I know this should be the last thing I'm doing, but he was so persistent and it would be nice to get out of my house and go out."

I watched my friends' reactions.

Penny pulled her hair back. "Okay, maybe we can all go out together, first."

Mia interrupted. "No, go out with Sullivan. He really seems okay."

"Mia?" Penny pressed.

"Penny?" Mia objected.

Erin let out a nervous laugh and twirled her straw in her frothy cup. "No, no, let's not overthink this. I mean, it's just one outing. Not a big deal."

Penny crossed her arms and leaned forward, her eyebrows raised. "Not a big deal? Erin, this is Sullivan we're talking about." Penny looked around the table. "Sullivan Farmer."

Erin sighed and stared back at Penny. "I know what he was like. But people can change, right? Can we agree that people can change? Besides, we've been working together and…he's been…different."

"I'm just in shock, that's all." Penny pressed.

"He's actually been nice," Erin replied softly. "Like, genuinely nice. He even offered to help me paint the backdrop after rehearsal next week."

"He's on the tech crew, he should be painting the backdrop." Penny caught herself. "I'm sorry, it's the shock talking."

Mia gave Erin an encouraging smile. "See? People can surprise you. Maybe he's trying."

"Or maybe he's just bored and trying to make himself look good," Penny countered. "Sorry, again—still in shock."

I glanced at my phone again, scrolling through messages. Still nothing from Sullivan. "Shouldn't he be here by now? What time did he say Ben was picking him up?"

Erin checked the clock on her phone. "He said around 6:30, and it's already 7:10."

Mia frowned and grabbed her phone. "I'll text him. Maybe Ben forgot."

"No!" Erin quickly interrupted, shaking her head. "I don't want him to think I'm panicking or something. He'll show up. Probably."

"Probably isn't reassuring," Penny muttered under her breath.

Mia ignored her and started typing anyway. "I'm just going to ask if everything's okay. It's not a big deal."

The table fell into an awkward silence, save for the soft clinking of Erin's straw against her cup. I kept refreshing my messages, the knot in my stomach tightening as each minute ticked by.

Penny leaned back in her chair, still unconvinced. "I don't know, Erin. Just...be careful, okay? I don't want you getting hurt."

"I'll be fine," Erin assured her, though her voice wavered slightly. "It's just one night."

"Yeah," Penny said quietly. "One night can be enough."

The tension lingered in the air as we all went back to our phones, waiting for Sullivan to finally show up.

Already knowing this information, I pulled out my phone to see if Sullivan had texted me. He hadn't.

Mia said, "He didn't text me back."

Mia reached over my arm to put her phone down when Erin screamed and knocked over her glass filled with her milkshake onto the table and then to the floor. I looked at Erin who was visibly alarmed. Her eyes seemed to have doubled in size as she stared across the table. Swiftly, she brought her hand to her mouth. She was making a grunting sound.

At this point, our waitress had made her way to our table with a large cloth towel. Erin slid herself out of her chair and walked to the corner of the restaurant. She moved in a gliding motion. Her hands that were once placed over her mouth, now hung at her side. Mia's eyes followed her.

My phone began to ring. I noticed Penny's phone, sitting on the table, light up. Mia's phone began to buzz, too. I grabbed Mia's hand under the table. Erin was still standing in the corner of the restaurant staring at the wall when she fainted and hit the floor of the restaurant. I hadn't picked up my phone yet, but I could see my dad was calling me.

Running over to Erin, I watched as the other customers sitting by where she fainted jumped up to her rescue. I stopped, turned around and answered my phone.

"Dad?" I answered as I swiped open my phone.

The customers and waitstaff of Puff Burgers had all surrounded Erin, who had now propped herself up on her elbows. She looked like she was giving some kind of direction to a customer who had her in their arms.

"Ty! Ty!" My dad was frantic on the phone. It was hard to hear him.

Mia ran over to me and grabbed my arm. "Ty!"

I was lost in the confusion of the chaos around me. Penny and Cali were on their phones as they ran to us.

I brought my phone back to my ear. "Dad, I'm here."

"Ty, there was an accident. There was a car accident." My phone buzzed now letting me know another caller was trying to reach me. My mom.

"Dad, Mom is calling me, too." I held the phone up to Mia to show her that I had two calls and that I was feeling overwhelmed.

"Ty, hang up with me and talk to your mom. Call me back," my dad insisted.

As I switched callers, I looked at Mia. She pulled on my shirt to bring my head down to her face. "Sullivan and Ben were in a car accident."

I pulled my head back up and switched my phone to my mom's call. "Mom! Mom!"

"Ty, I just got a call from Allie's mom. She said that there was a car accident, but she didn't give me any more information. She did know it involved kids from school." She was breathless as she spoke. "Who is with you at the restaurant?"

I was trying to stay focused on my conversation with my mom while watching Penny and Cali help Erin.

My mom repeated, "Ty, who is with you?"

I came back to the call. "Uh, Mia, Erin, Penny, and Cali, and Sullivan is on his way."

Erin must've heard me and swung her body around, allowing Penny to help her up. Erin's skin was gray and ashen. She pushed herself off of Penny and with determination marched over to me. She pulled my arm and dragged me back to our table.

"Mom, I'll call you back," I ended the phone call.

We stood at the table. The smell of the grilling burgers made me nauseous. I thought I was about to get sick. Erin looked me right in the eyes. She began to breathe heavily as if she had run a mile. Her eyes were wide and wet.

"What?!" I was flooded by the smell of the greasy fries and the sweet, melting milkshakes that were still sitting on the table.

"Erin, WHAT?" I demanded.

The waitstaff of the restaurant had circled the table. I was sure they were interested in knowing that Erin was okay. I could see her hand was bleeding where she may have hit the floor. Mia, Penny, and Cali came back and stood over the table too. Penny put a hand over her mouth.

"Listen to me, Ty," Erin begged. "My dad is here. My dad's here! I haven't seen or shadowed with him in over a year."

Penny couldn't keep her hand from expelling some noises. I noticed Cali turn to the waitress in what seemed to be a motion to move her away and explain that everything is going to be fine.

"Erin, I need you to finish your thought," I said firmly, getting louder. One reason was because her actions were frightening me and the second was because the restaurant had not quieted.

"My dad came back to bring someone to me," Erin began to cry. "Ty, my dad was bringing me Sullivan."

Penny's sobs were noticeable to the others in the restaurant. Mia lost her balance and slid into the chair underneath her. Erin and I kept a gaze on each other. I couldn't move.

My phone began to buzz and I saw it was my dad calling me. I swiped open. "Dad?" Erin didn't take her eyes off of me.

Mia had placed her head on my shoulder and was crying. Penny had walked away in tears. Cali followed.

"Ty, I'm on my way to you, but the traffic has slowed down for emergency vehicles." His voice was calm. "I spoke to mom and she knows I'm on my way."

"Okay, Dad." I couldn't give him any more than that.

Erin began to talk, still staring into my eyes. She was afraid to look away as to what she might see. "My dad is standing by the window."

Instinctively, I turned my head to the window at the back of the restaurant. I looked over a sea of customer's heads. I didn't see him.

"He's looking at me, but I can't look back." Erin wiped her tears that had rolled onto her cheeks with the back of her hand. "He wants to bring me Sullivan."

I felt like I was about to faint. I gripped onto the

chair I was sitting in for support. Mia picked her head up to look at me. I looked back over to the window where Erin said her dad was standing. The neon lights cast an eerie hue over the window, but I didn't see anyone there. The door of the restaurant flew open and I saw Michelle and my dad enter together. They scanned the restaurant for us. As they noticed us sitting there, Talia walked in followed by Penny and Cali's moms. Audible gasps and cries were heard as the parents walked to their kids.

Erin and I continued the long stare at each other. Talia approached the table and picked up Erin's army green bag, now covered in the milkshake she ordered. Talia placed a gentle hand on Erin's shoulder.

Erin turned up to her mom. "Dad's here."

Talia curled her bottom lip under her top two front teeth and nodded. My dad stood behind me and waited. Mia had gotten up to meet Michelle in a tight embrace. The restaurant was either very quiet now or I blocked it out, but nothing seemed to be distracting me.

As we left, each of us held onto one another. In the distance I could hear the sounds of police cars and ambulances. Mia and I held onto each other in the longest grip. How were we supposed to move forward from here?

15

Sullivan's death was devastating. His funeral was standing room only. It was filled with students he knew and didn't know, teachers he had and didn't have, and many people from the community. My mom had said when a young person dies, there are more people to mourn the loss than someone who is very old. This seemed very true.

Sullivan's father spoke. He was stoic as he stood in front of the gathering of people, but he spoke of his son in a way like no one else could. I looked at him to see if he showed any signs of being ill. He looked thin and tired, but that would have been expected at this moment.

He described Sullivan as headstrong and opinionated. He shared his love of sports and music and horror movies. He told stories of family vacations they took together with Sullivan in the back of the car shouting cliche phrases, like, "Are we almost there?" and "I'm hungry!" The members of the congregation nodded their heads as Mr. Farmer spoke.

Sullivan's sister, Natalie, spoke too. I had never met her before. She, too, was soft spoken, but at moments had times when she had to stop to catch her breath. She held a tissue in her hand and moved it across her eyes and under her nose. Her words about her brother's life made you really understand how in love and devoted this family was to each other.

Once the service ended, Mia and I had shifted our way through the crowd of people to get close to Sullivan's family. Ben looked weak. He was in two casts. One on his left arm and one on his right leg. Sullivan's father pushed Ben in a wheelchair. As Sullivan's dad stepped away to talk to a guest, Mia and I moved toward Ben.

"Ben, I don't know if you remember me. Ty Steiner." My voice clutched in my throat as Ben looked up and nodded. Mia held onto my hand.

"Thanks for coming." Those were the only words Ben got out before he started to cry. Mia and I got down on our knees to be closer to him. "Sullivan was really excited about being a part of the play at school," he whispered.

"I know." Mia agreed with Ben. "He was really happy to be there."

"Please make sure that you continue it. Don't stop

the production." Ben was overcome with emotion. "My family and I want the show to go on. We were just talking about it today with the drama teacher. He was here today, too."

16

THE CURTAIN FELL ONTO THE stage as the cast of *Guys and Dolls* took their bows. I was standing between Mia and Allie holding onto each of their hands as we stood onstage looking into the theater. The curtain began to drop and we took a step back. The audience's applause and cheers were muffled and softened, shielded by the thick red curtain. As the curtain hit the stage, the cast members began to disperse across the stage. It was then that I heard Mr. Bronson begin to talk to the audience on the microphone. He stood on the other side of the curtain. In his speech, he thanked the cast for coming together and creating an amazing performance. He continued to thank the audience for coming and sharing our story. Then he paused. It was incredibly quiet on stage and in the theater.

"This show has been dedicated to our student, Sullivan Farmer." Mr. Bronson cleared his throat. "Sullivan came to me a few months ago to tell me that he wanted to be a part of the technical crew for this show." Mr. Bronson's words filled the theater. I was still holding onto Mia's hand. A tearful Allie had moved to the dressing rooms.

"I want the cast, crew, and audience to know how much joy Sullivan found in the short time he was involved with this show." Bronson paused. "His family came to me and insisted that we continue *Guys and Dolls* to honor Sullivan."

I turned to Mia and squeezed her hand. I knew what was next.

Mr. Bronson finished. "Ty Steiner, who played Nathan Detroit, would like to speak about his friend, Sullivan Farmer."

Mia released my hand as I turned to walk around the back of the curtain to meet Mr. Bronson in front. Behind me, Mia, Erin, and Penny followed. I took the hat off I was wearing and looked out into the audience. It was very difficult to see any faces as the stage lights were shining brightly. I knew that Sullivan's family was here. I made sure to look in the direction to where I thought they were sitting.

"Thank you for coming to tonight's show. The cast, as well as Mr. Bronson and the entire crew, are so thankful." I could hear sniffing and sighing around me and in the theater. I reached into the side pocket of the jacket I was wearing to pull out the notes I had written. I opened up the papers. "My name is Ty Steiner and I have known Sullivan Farmer for a long time.

"Ask me how do I feel, and I will tell you that Sullivan was a powerful energy in our lives. He brought a warmth, pulling in all those fortunate enough to know him. Sullivan's laughter and genuine smile could light up any room, bringing comfort and happiness to those around him. Sullivan didn't let you get away with anything." I paused and laughed a bit. "He knew how to call you out on something. He knew what to say and sometimes what not to say." Some members of the cast agreed with a soft laugh.

"Ask me how do I feel, and I will tell you that Sullivan had a profound impact on us. Like the sound of a ringing bell, in the last few months, he brought people together, with love and acceptance."

I turned to Erin, whose face was looking down at her feet, but when I paused in my speech, she looked up at me, and then something caught her attention out in the audience. I knew she was looking at someone I couldn't see.

Erin's Journal

When Ty spoke, it was like Sullivan's voice was moving between his words. "Ask me how do

I feel..." The memories of Sullivan's laughter, his brutal honesty, his way of seeing straight through people. I could see the way his energy had touched every person in the theater, from Ty bravely holding back tears to the cast chuckling softly at the truth in his words. But Sullivan wasn't always that person. In his early years, he wasn't warm or kind. He was sharp and cutting. He was a bully who thrived on pointing out weaknesses and turning them into jokes for everyone else. I still remember the day it all came to a head. I hated it, though. It felt like I'd lost everything because of him. And now? Now I can say I barely recognize the boy he used to be in the spirit standing before me.

People change, I know that, but having seen him tonight, hearing Ty speak about his warmth and laughter, it's still hard to piece together the Sullivan I knew. And then I saw them. His family. Sitting in the shadows of the theater, holding onto each other, their grief painted across their faces. My chest tightened. Sullivan stood behind them, his hand was resting lightly on his mom's shoulder.

When Ty paused and looked at me, I looked right into his eyes and then I slowly moved my gaze and looked right at Sullivan. I wanted Ty to know that he was here. That I saw him here. When I caught Sullivan's eyes, his gaze wasn't heavy or sad, it was *knowing. Like he understood everything I felt and wanted me to know it was okay, that he was okay, and I felt it. I wanted to say something to his family, let them know that he's still here, still watching, still loving them. But instead, I just stood there, covered in the stage light, locked in this moment feeling the gravity of his presence. The pull and the push of him being here. Also the bittersweetness of knowing I could see him when they couldn't. Sometimes, seeing and speaking to the dead feels like a gift. Other times, it feels like a burden I'll never quite understand. Tonight, it felt like both.*

ACKNOWLEDGMENTS

Yael, your love, patience, and unwavering support have been the foundation of this journey. Your late night burning of the midnight oil, reading and editing this story has me in awe of you.

Harris Fishman, Sam Fishman, Taylor Barth, Angela Alejo, Lynne Schreer, Dean Fishman, Laura Fishman, Harriet Gerstenfeld, Luisa Feinglass, Beth Millman, Lori Wolk, Melanie Diamond, Amanda Fursetzer, Hope Kennedy, Rachel Feiman, Rita Vester, Tayna Lynch, Liz Korkoz, Melissa Clark, Eileen Feldsott, and Ysa Ortiz. Your insight, patience, and belief in me have been invaluable.

Thank you to my grandmother, Helen Fishman, who shared her love of the music from *Guys and Dolls*, which she played on her record player in her apartment while I was a child. This is a memory I will always treasure.

I am profoundly grateful to the students of North Broward Preparatory High School: Jake Clayman,

Alyssa DeCross, Christopher Evans, Kate Lynch, Colette Marquez, Lola Rubin, and Ellie Street for generously sharing their insights into life as a high school student. The time you spent reading, editing, and offering thoughtful suggestions was nothing short of amazing!

A heartfelt thank you to my publisher, Daniel Brantley from Argyle Fox publishing, for your support and belief in this story. I'm thankful for your commitment to helping me share my story. Your guidance has been invaluable.

I'm forever grateful to all of you for helping me bring *Ask Me How Do I Feel* off my computer and into your hands.

9 798891 240742